Mountain Haven

Mountain Mayhem Series - One

Dawn Love

Dawn Love

"The mightiest power of death is not that it can make people die, but that it can make the people you left behind want to stop living."
— **Fredrik Backman,** My Grandmother Asked Me to Tell You She's Sorry

Copyright © 2022 by Dawn Love

All rights reserved.

The characters and events portrayed in this book are fictitious. Any similarity to real persons, living or dead, is coincidental and not intended by the author.

No part of this book may be reproduced, or stored in a retrieval system, or transmitted in any form or by any means, electronic, mechanical, photocopying, recording, or otherwise, without express written permission of the publisher.

Photographer: FuriousFotog

Cover Model: Matthew Hosea

Cover Design: FuriousFotog

Printed in the United States of America.

Content/Trigger Warnings

Mountain Haven is meant for adults and contains explicit and graphic sexual scenes and language; themes of grief, death, infant loss, loss of fertility; mental illness, PTSD, depression, agoraphobia; violence; stalking; attempted kidnapping; and disturbing imagery. It is this author's intent to never cause harm or distress with her words. If ever you feel that there should be a warning about any subject or scene in her work, please reach out to her through her social media or email.

https://linktr.ee/dawnlove

Dedication

For anyone who has ever had their entire life mapped out only to find that fate has set up a detour and rerouted you on the road to your final destination.

Contents

Chapter One	1
Chapter Two	17
Chapter Three	30
Chapter Four	45
Chapter Five	63
Chapter Six	85
Chapter Seven	112
Chapter Eight	137
Chapter Nine	156
Chapter Ten	174
Chapter Eleven	189
Chapter Twelve	202

Chapter Thirteen	220
Epilogue	242
More by Dawn Love	248
Acknowledgments	250
About the Author	252

Chapter One

Sometimes you wish hard enough, long enough, desperately enough for something, that your wish comes true. Other times, no matter how hard you wish, no matter how much you long for it, it remains just out of reach, yet still on the horizon. And then, there are those times that what you wish for, what you need, and what your heart longingly breaks for, can never happen because what you desire no longer exists.

These thoughts swirled through Lexi's mind as she stood on her mountaintop in the brisk early morning air and looked out over the trees, across the nearby mountains and valleys, and reminisced about the highs and lows of her life, the good times and the bad. At twenty-nine she'd experienced her fair share of highs and, much to her dismay, more than her fair share of lows.

She'd grown up in the heart of western Kentucky, a fun-loving country girl who'd tromped through the fields and woods that had surrounded her house with gleeful abandon, climbed trees like a monkey, and waded through the local creek barefoot. She'd gone to the bonfires and pep rallies in high school and then sat in the stands as a member of the marching band and cheered on the football team as they'd played their hearts out in hopes of a state championship.

Her daddy had taught her to shoot a rifle and how to change a tire; her momma had taught her how to cook, bake and sew. She'd loved to camp and fish, spending her summers on Kentucky Lake enjoying the outdoors, but she'd also loved to dress up, throw on some high heels and hang out at school dances while she drove the local boys crazy.

She'd gone out with her friends on Friday and Saturday nights and come Sunday morning she'd parked her butt in a church pew to listen to the hellfire and brimstone sermons the pastor was famous for, whether she'd really wanted to or not. You were just as likely to have seen her riding in the back of a pickup truck as you would the snappy little convertible she'd talked her parents into buying for her sixteenth birthday.

All in all, her upbringing had made her a loveable, well-rounded person, and her positive personality and outlook on life had drawn people to her like flies to honey.

When she'd realized that her vocal talent and passion for singing could lead to a music career, she'd done everything she could to make a name for herself. She'd sang at church, she'd sang with the garage band she'd thrown together, and when she'd been old enough, she'd sang on stage in all the local bars.

Word had gotten out and by the time she was twenty-one she'd started traveling with a band performing country music throughout the mid-west; by twenty-three she'd moved to Nashville and signed a recording contract with a major record label.

She had taken to stardom like a fish to water and she'd navigated her way through the music scene with ease. Through it all, she'd had her best friend, Jackson, by her side. He had been her friend, her lover, and had fate not screwed her over, he would have been her happily ever after, husband and father to the children she had wanted for as long as she could remember.

Fate, she thought, could be a cold and cruel bitch.

They'd met in middle school and their friendship had been instant and intense, and they'd shared an unbreakable bond. Then one night, after a school dance during their freshman year of high school, they'd sat on the front porch swing of her parents' farmhouse, and he'd made his move.

The kiss had been tentative, soft, and sweet, a first for both. He'd sat back and looked at her, his eyes questioning if he'd gone too far, and she'd smiled at him in reassurance before leaning into him for another kiss, deeper, longer, and heart-stopping.

He'd asked her to be his girlfriend before he'd left that night, and without hesitation, she'd said yes. They'd dated from that point forward, never a hint of breaking up. They'd laughed and loved like they'd had all the time in the world. When they'd lost their innocence to each other at the tender age of seventeen, she'd known they were truly meant to be, fated, eternal love.

As they'd claimed each other on a blanket at the water's edge of the local swimming hole that night, crickets chirping, frogs croaking, the clear night sky full of stars close enough to reach out and touch, she'd seen their future. A beautiful wedding surrounded by their friends and family, a little house on a hill with a yard large enough to hold their three children and a dog or two.

A wide front porch with a wooden rocker and a white bench swing swaying in the breeze as a cat curled up for a nap, ignoring the chaos of the running children and barking dogs. And when they were older, much older, there would be grandchildren and great-grandchildren on that porch rocking in her arms.

Yes, she'd seen how it could have been. How it should have been.

He'd gone to college while she'd been forging her path in the music world. And when the music had eventually drawn her to Nashville, he'd gone with her. No questions asked, just full, unbending support, a lifeline as she'd navigated those murky waters in her rise to fame.

While their relationship hadn't been perfect, it had been close. They'd argued - all couples argue at some point, she thought, but their arguments had been minor and easily resolved.

They'd rented an apartment, their first place together, and while he'd worked days clerking at a small law firm, she'd worked nights, belting her songs at every bar and local artists' venues in the Nashville area.

She'd spent her days in the recording studio putting together her debut album and when her first single had hit the airwaves, she'd become an overnight success, instant stardom. It hadn't been long until talk of a tour had come about and Jackson had shared her excitement at the possibilities laid out before them, the potential for their future.

The night before the first leg of the tour he'd surprised her with a candlelight dinner, had gotten on one knee and proposed while slipping a golden band with a sparkling pear-shaped diamond onto her finger. There were no words in her mind to describe just how perfect the moment had been, and she'd given him a resounding 'yes' in response.

She'd taken off the next morning with jittery nerves fluttering through her body, excited to be officially on tour, but apprehensive at the thought of being away from Jackson for the first time. But they'd made it through the tearful goodbye and the anxiety of separation, with long late-night phone calls filled with love and promises for their future.

She'd finished the first leg of her tour on a high note. Venues had sold out; fans had cheered and sang along. There had been "meet & greets" where she'd signed autographs until her hand had cramped and posed for photo after photo, always happy to see the fans who were thrilled at the opportunity to meet her. She couldn't have imagined life being any better at that point apart from the aching loneliness that had left her hollow and empty with the absence of the man she loved.

There had been a two-week break between the first and second half of the tour and when Jackson had met her at the airport, a dozen long-stemmed yellow roses in hand, she'd run to him and jumped in his arms, holding tightly and kissing him passionately while the world around them had faded away with their reunion. They'd rushed home, rushed to bed, and then slowed everything down as they'd loved, exploring each other's bodies as if it were the first time all over again.

Two weeks had passed in a blur and then she'd been on the road again. Knowing that it would be a long time before they'd be together and remembering how they'd missed each other with the first separation, had led to another tearful goodbye, heart-wrenching once again.

As her plane had taxied down the runway, she'd reminded herself that the sooner she left and took care of business, the sooner she'd return to Nashville and to Jackson and the life they were building. Then she would be able to have a nice break before returning to the studio, and with any luck, she'd then be able to concentrate her time on planning their wedding.

She'd just stepped off stage after the final concert of the tour when she'd received the phone call that had caused her world to shatter and come crashing down around her. There'd been a wreck.

A car had lost control and ended up careening off into the Cumberland River. Jackson, being the wonderful, caring man he had always been, had, without a thought for his own safety, jumped in the river to try to help. Both he and the driver had drowned when Jackson had gotten caught under debris while trying to save him.

Devastated and in disbelief, she'd decided to leave Nashville and much to everyone's dismay, to leave the music world behind. She'd no longer felt the lyrics, the melodies and harmonies within. Her internal song had died when Jackson had died. She'd bought her way out of her music contract and returned to Kentucky, staying with her parents while she'd grieved, while she'd tried to sort out the scrambled pieces of her life.

Nightmares had plagued her, visions of her future with Jackson that had been so clear and concise, perfect, were put together and ripped apart night after night. She'd woken screaming, crying uncontrollably, and her mother had rushed to her room time and again to hold her and offer comfort.

Gradually, the intensity of the pain had lessened, but it had still been there, and would always be there, she thought. She'd known that Jackson wouldn't have wanted her to continue to mourn, but to pick herself up, dust herself off, and begin to live again. So, several months later she'd begun trying to figure out where she wanted to go and what she wanted to do. It was at that point that fate, that cruel, hateful bitch, had stepped in again. Her parents had gone out to dinner one night and had never returned. They'd died in a head-on collision with a drunk driver.

At that point she'd become numb, detached, and apathetic to the world she'd been thrust into. She'd been hollowed out and had become a shell of the person she had once been. The light within that had burned so brightly had been snuffed out, and she'd wanted nothing more than to hide from everyone and everything for the rest of her life.

Total devastation smothered her with a cloak of darkness. Everyone she'd ever loved had been taken from her. Alone, she'd had no idea where to turn nor what to do. Day after day, night after night, she'd sat and stared into space, dazed, confused, with no direction, no hope. Lost.

Then one day she'd found her escape. With the sale of her parent's estate and royalties from her album, she'd bought her property high in the mountains and built her house, built her haven, her refuge. Living on a mountaintop became her line of defense against the world – she could see everything coming at her from any direction she looked.

The mountains of West Virginia weren't where she'd envisioned herself all those years ago, but it was home now, where she felt safe, secure, and where she intended to live out the remainder of her days. Peaceful solitude was her lifeline.

She had nothing but memories, little moments in time forever frozen in her mind, her heart, of the way things had been. But she held on to each and every mental snapshot as they kept her loved ones alive, kept her alive – perfectly etched images of a beautiful life shattered by tragedy.

Shaking herself back to the present, she sniffed the cold mountain air and studied the darkening sky, shivering lightly in her thick winter coat as the wind picked up bringing bracing gusts out of the north. There will be snow before morning she thought and began a rundown of the list of things she needed to do before the storm hit.

Living in the mountains had quickly taught her that you had to be attuned to the weather and the rapid changes that seemingly appeared out of nowhere. After almost five years, she felt she had gotten good at predicting changes, preparing, and adapting. She turned, and with one last look at the vast, seemingly endless beauty before her, hiked back down the mountain to start tackling the chores for what promised to be a very long day ahead.

He maneuvered the truck back and forth through yet another switchback. The narrow mountain road he'd been climbing for the past couple of hours had twisted and turned, rising up the steep terrain, a snake climbing a rocky hillside. The beauty of the skyline, distant mountains rising and falling on the horizon, thrilled, even as it brought him a sense of peace that he'd not felt in years.

It seemed as if he'd been in the mountains for days rather than a few hours, and the twists and turns that had his foot moving from brake to gas and back to brake were invigorating and exhausting at the same time. He was enjoying the drive, but what had begun as a cool, breezy day had quickly turned blustery and bitterly cold. The higher he climbed, the more the gusts of wind rocked the truck.

The cloudy and overcast sky that had started the day had turned into a gray haze that promised a quick and heavy snowfall. The first flakes had drifted beautifully, enchanting him as they'd softly floated in a sprinkling of crystals and melted on the defrosted heat of the windshield. What had been light and fluffy was now coming down so hard and with such speed that the road visibility had become difficult.

He found he was thankful for the four-wheel drive of his truck as the wheels safely dug ruts into the mushy snow as he climbed higher and higher. Seeing that the roads were steadily getting worse, he gradually slowed to a crawl but continued his journey up the mountain.

When the storm had picked up, he'd been fairly certain that he was getting close to the peak, and it had made more sense to him to continue over the mountaintop rather than turn around. But now as he squinted through the dizzying star-field of flakes, the quick swish of the wiper blades, he was second-guessing himself and his once infallible intuition.

He chuckled as he realized how badly he'd misjudged the trip. When at last he finally topped the mountain and started on the road down the other side, relief washed through him. And as he drove over the peak, he noticed the long, deep cut of a driveway that meandered up the mountain, weaving its way through the trees and brush up to a rustic-looking log cabin.

The rich amber wood of the two-story A-frame blended so well with its surroundings, even in the bareness of winter, that it appeared as if it was a natural part of the landscape. The mountain crested gently, rising behind the cabin and lovingly framing it. Longing surged through him.

That was what he wanted, exactly what he wanted. A place in the mountains, a place away from everyone and everything. A place to escape, a place for solitude, and at long last, a place to deal with all the hellish demons that constantly chased him in a race to possess his soul.

He'd been away too damn long and was more than ready to get back to his roots.

He'd grown up in rural West Virginia, his family having lived there for several generations. He'd done all the normal things a country boy did as he'd grown up – played on a little league team, rode horses, and spent his nights chugging beer and chasing local girls in hopes to get laid as often as possible. He'd not really had any ambition to speak of, no more than getting a piece of ass or two, and when he'd entered his senior year of high school it had been with the unsettling knowledge that he had no idea what to do with his life.

With his diploma in hand, he'd walked across the graduation stage, pausing only long enough to look out on the sea of faces in the audience. It was in that moment that it had dawned on him that the best option for his future at that point in his life had been to join the military.

Shortly after graduation he'd walked into the Navy recruiter's office and signed his name on the paperwork that gave him freedom and a path to follow at the same time it tied him down and gave him a foundation. He'd served his time and then some, re-enlisting and working his way up through the ranks before eventually joining up with a Special Forces unit. The things he'd seen and done, had been forced to do in the unit, would haunt him until his dying breath.

For years he'd gone into foreign countries, invaded bunkers, and helped to take down corrupt and oppressive governments, and hate-filled and controlling factions. Everything he'd done had been an attempt to free the people being held back, held down, raped, tortured, and murdered on a daily basis. Eventually, it had become more than his conscience could carry. The horror of what he'd done, what he'd had to do, though it had been done in the name of freedom and justice, had begun to weigh on him with each new assignment.

He'd needed out, needed peace, quiet, and something else, something more, something the military would not and could not ever give him. And though he wasn't entirely certain what that something else was just yet, he was determined to find it, determined to grab on to whatever it was and never let go. He just hoped that whatever it ended up being would help him sort through the restlessness, through the unsettling feeling that he'd somehow made a wrong turn in life.

He'd flown in from California the day before and had crashed in his hotel room almost as soon as he'd walked in the door, the ink on his discharge papers and stamp on his passport still wet. He'd fallen face first on the queen-sized mattress and slept for fourteen hours straight, a testament to his exhaustion, mental and physical.

He'd gotten up that morning, found a car dealership, and had taken the first step toward making his move back home, back to a life of normalcy, or, at least, to what he sincerely hoped and prayed would be a normal life. Yes, he'd signed his name on a dotted line and changed his life once again.

The shiny red and chrome of his new 4 x 4 wasn't quite so shiny after a day of driving through slushy mountain roads. Snow-encrusted dirt clung to the undercarriage and spattered in the wheel wells. A thick film covered his headlights, but even as filthy as his new toy was, it still gave him a little thrill to think he'd bought his first car in more years than he could count. There hadn't been a need for one while he'd been in the military. It had been easy enough to get around the bases he'd been stationed at without one, and when he'd joined the Special Ops, there'd been no reason to bother.

He'd never been in one place more than a few weeks at a time after that, going from one assignment to another in the blink of an eye. He'd had to be ready to move out at a moment's notice, day or night, packing all his belongings in a duffel bag and hot-footing it to his next location. It was a life he was glad to be leaving behind. He only wished he knew for sure where the life ahead of him was determined to take him next.

He glanced out the side of the truck as he rounded the next curve, his mind wandering, and when he looked back, he was met with the startled onyx eyes of the largest buck he'd ever seen.

One moment the road had been empty, the next his view out of the windshield had been entirely blocked by the deer, a massive head and body loaded with heavy, snow-encrusted antlers. He swerved to miss it and when he did, the truck skid uncontrollably and slammed into the side of the mountain. As the front corner of his bumper crumpled from the impact, the airbag deployed, hitting him in the face, snapping his head back with flashing, searing pain, and knocking him out.

The buck, unaware of the events he'd just set in motion with his sudden appearance, quickly and quietly leapt away.

Chapter Two

Lexi was carrying her second load of firewood inside when she heard the boom from the crash. Her heart jumped at the unfamiliar sound, and she found herself looking around to determine from which direction it had come. Though she knew there'd been no change in the weather, she looked up at the sky, hopeful that she wouldn't have to investigate and deal with the intrusion. Sighing as she saw no possible relief in sight, she grudgingly made the decision to go see what had happened.

She stomped her boots, dislodging snow as she crossed the wide front porch of her home and hurried inside to add the load of wood she carried to the pile by the fireplace. She grabbed the keys to her Gator and rushed out to the shed. She quickly made her way down the drive and then not knowing for sure which direction to go, mentally flipped a coin and headed to the right.

She didn't have to go far before she saw the truck. The front end was smashed into the side of the mountain and angled head-first into a ditch while the back end sat with the left wheel in the air. Great, she thought, whoever it is will have to be pulled out.

She glanced at the sky again and shook her head. They were definitely going to need a wrecker, but there was no way it was happening anytime soon. It was getting dark and with the way the snow was coming down, the road would be impassable for a couple of days, at the very least.

She hurried over to the driver's side and peered in. She decided luck was on her side when she realized there was only one person in the vehicle. Whoever he was, he was going to have to hunker down with her for a couple of days. She rapped her knuckles on the window to try to get his attention, but the guy was out cold. She tried again and again, but he didn't respond.

She pulled on the door handle only to find the door locked. Damn it, she thought as she hurried back over to the gator and searched for something to help get her in the truck. She decided luck was on her side when she grabbed onto the hammer she'd left laying on the floorboard from where she'd been making a repair earlier that morning to the fence around her goat pen.

She went back to the window and tried once again to get his attention, but he was still unresponsive. While she hated to break the glass, they needed to get back to the house soon. The storm had quickly become more intense and was well on its way to reaching whiteout conditions. It took her a couple of good swings, but she managed to break the side window and unlock and open the driver's door.

She shook him a few times and when she got the first moan of response, she began talking to him.

"Hey! I need you to wake up now." She shook him again. "Come on, man. You've got to get awake enough to get over to the Gator. I can help you, but I sure as hell can't carry you."

Blaze blinked his eyes a few times and tried to focus. For some reason, he was seeing two of everything. Someone was talking to him, but he was having trouble figuring out where the voice was coming from. After a moment he slowly became aware of his surroundings, and as he looked to his left, he could have sworn he saw an angel. Well, damn, he thought, I'm dead. It was the only explanation he could come up with in his confusion.

In the back of his mind, he realized she was trying to help him, to get him out of the truck, and somehow his muscles began to cooperate even though his brain was having a hard time making sense of what was happening. Wincing against the pain and confusion, and struggling to make sense of what was happening, he slowly began walking. With her help he stumbled over to the small car she drove, and when he did, he had a quick fractured thought that it was an odd little car.

He slid into the passenger seat, leaned his head against a railing, and began to shiver in the freezing cold. He heard the growl of the engine increase as they started moving, but he didn't have another coherent thought until he felt her urging him out of the seat, up a set of stairs, and into golden light and blessed warmth.

Lexi helped him onto the couch and stood looking down at him as she tried to figure out just what to do with him. It had been quite a struggle to get his large frame into the Gator and from the Gator to her couch. He had a gash on his forehead, and if she'd understood his mumblings correctly, she was fairly certain he had a concussion. She only knew first aid basics, but felt she needed to help as best she could and set about making him as comfortable as possible.

She took his shit-kicker boots off him and hefted his long legs up onto the armrest. His tall muscular body was more than her couch could handle and his feet dangled off the end. Realizing there wasn't much she could do about that, Lexi grabbed a blanket and tucked it around him before going to retrieve some medical supplies to clean his head wound.

The savory aroma of vegetable soup permeated the air as Blaze slowly became aware of his surroundings. His head hurt like a son-of-a-bitch and his body felt like he'd been on a three-day bender, his muscles tender and achy. He slowly opened his eyes, blinked a few times, and tried to figure out exactly where he was, and how exactly he'd gotten there. A stone fireplace radiated welcome warmth from a blazing fire as well as a cozy glow that glistened off the homey walls of the room.

He sat up quickly, too quickly, and had his head spinning. Wishing he could just remove the damn thing from his body, he groaned and held on with both hands hoping it would help the tilt-a-whirl he suddenly found himself on.

He sensed more than heard someone come up behind him and years of training kicked in jack-knifing his body off the couch and into a defensive position. When he saw startled and wary eyes looking him over, he slowly let down his guard.

"Who the hell are you and where the hell am I?"

"I'm Lexi Lane and you're in my house. Do you want to tell me who you are?"

"Blaze. Michael Blaisure, but everybody calls me Blaze. What am I doing here?"

"Well, the best I can tell you decided to see how well your truck could handle being a wrecking ball. Do you remember playing bumper cars and smashing into the side of the mountain?"

"No. Wait." His head pounded as flashes of the giant buck came hurtling through his memory. "Shit. Yeah. A deer, big fu-- ah, sucker, jumped out in front of me. I swerved and that's about all I remember."

"I heard the crash and went to investigate. I found you out cold. I guess the airbag did the damage to your head." She pointed to the white bandage she'd carefully applied after she'd cleaned and tended to his wound. "Why don't you sit down? Because I swear to you that if you faint, I'm leaving you where you fall. You're too damn big for me to get you back on the couch."

"I'm not going to faint." At least he hoped like hell he wouldn't. He sat back down and tried to take stock of his injuries, wincing at the throbbing pain. "My head is exploding."

"I'm pretty sure you have a concussion. I'm going to get you some aspirin."

"Bring the whole damn bottle, ok?"

She laughed softly. "How about some soup, too? You've been out of it for several hours now. It might be wise to put some food in you before we load you up with too many drugs."

His stomach growled as he once again sniffed the air. "Yeah. That would be great. Thank you."

She disappeared around the corner into what he assumed was the kitchen. And when she was out of sight, he leaned back on the couch, resting his head on the back cushion, and closed his eyes.

Fuck, fuck, fuck! He couldn't believe he'd wrecked his new truck and his head felt like a damn bomb had gone off in it. He reached up and gingerly felt the bandage. He guessed he owed her a debt of gratitude. He very easily could still have been sitting on the side of the road in the freezing cold rather than in her warm home being treated to her hospitality.

She's a beauty, he thought. All that curling mass of red hair was enough to drive a man crazy. Her hazel green eyes were mesmerizing, and her top-heavy mouth made a man want to dive in and stay awhile. It dawned on him as he raised his head and looked around that her home must be the A-frame that he'd seen sitting atop the mountain. It was just as breathtaking inside as it was out, and a vague thought trickled through his mind that he wondered if he could talk her into selling.

She came around the corner with a tray holding a steaming bowl of soup, what he supposed was a glass of tea, and a large bottle of aspirin.

"Thank you. Thank you for helping me out of the wreck and for this," he pointed to his head. "I really do appreciate it. The meal, too."

"Well, I couldn't very well leave you out there. You'll have to get a tow. There's no way you'll be able to get the truck out on your own." Although she thought, looking at all his bulging muscles outlined beneath the covering of a long-sleeved t-shirt, she wouldn't put it past him to just pull it out under his own power.

He spooned up his first bite of soup as he asked, "Would you happen to have the number for a towing service?" He took the bite and felt his body go lax with pleasure. "Oh my God. This is excellent."

"Thanks. Yeah, I can get you the number, but you aren't going anywhere for at least a couple of days."

"What? Why?"

"I guess you haven't looked outside yet. We've got about six inches on the ground and it's still coming down hard. We may end up with a foot of snow before things settle down out there. So, unless you want to camp out in your truck for a couple of days, welcome to home away from home."

Lexi walked over to the floor-to-ceiling windows and shifted the heavy curtain to the side so he could peer out. Disbelief crossed his face as he stared out at the winter wonderland before him. Her porch was dotted with solar lights that were close to being buried underneath drifts of heavy snow. The soft glow reflected on piles of white that seemed to get deeper by the second. "Well, shit. I hate to impose this way, but if you're okay with it, I appreciate it."

"I wouldn't say I'm okay with it, but I'm not heartless, and you really don't have much choice." Sadness crossed her features as she continued, "Besides, everyone needs a safe haven once in a while." She walked back over and studied him as he began eating again. "What on earth had you driving up this way when a snowstorm was about to hit?"

He thought as he swallowed, trying to come up with a good answer and deciding quickly that a half-truth was better than a complete lie. "First, I didn't realize a storm was coming. Second, I'm looking for property." Not running away, he thought, not trying to hide from the world. No, not that. "I'm hoping to build a home similar to what you have here. At least as far as location. I want something where I can enjoy some peace and quiet. I uh, I don't suppose you know of any land for sale around here, do you?"

"I'm afraid I don't keep up with those sorts of things. I rarely leave the mountain. Sorry."

He continued eating and echoing silence stretched between them. When he'd finished, he shook a few aspirin from the bottle and praying that they helped to ease the ache in his head, washed them down with the cool, sweet tea. "Thank you again for your hospitality." He started to rise to carry the tray to the kitchen, but she waved him back down to the couch.

"No. Sit. I've got this." She carted the tray around the corner, and he couldn't help but watch her until she disappeared from sight. The body-hugging jeans she wore left little to the imagination yet had his imagination working overtime. He heard her cleaning up, setting her kitchen to rights, and once again took in his surroundings.

Giant bookcases sat on either side of the fireplace and were packed full of books, two rows deep and without an inch to spare. Everything from Austen to King and more adorned the shelves - classics, mysteries, horror, science fiction, and romance. Obviously, she was an avid reader, or someone who lived in the house was, he thought, as she hadn't actually told him if she lived alone or not.

Restless, he walked to the shelf and picked up a well-worn copy of All Quiet on the Western Front. He'd read the book a couple of times himself. Flashes of war, pain, suffering, and despair, ran through his mind, shaking loose a few of the demons he carried with him. They taunted him from the edges of his memory, swirling black masses with laughing red eyes. They screamed at him that he could have done things differently, that he should have done things differently. And with each scene that replayed, they showed him exactly how he'd fucked up.

He felt himself starting to slide down the slope of despair and found himself having to take a deep breath so as to not lose his grip on reality.

He shook his head and quickly put the book back as he mentally lassoed the little horned devils, tucking them away to be dealt with another time. He stuck his hands in his jean pockets and began to slowly wander about the large room.

There was no television, no stereo that he could see, which he found odd, but simply shrugged off as eccentricity. He took in the soft beige carpet that ran from wall to wall, the simple yet elegant furniture, but was drawn to a wall full of paintings.

Beautiful abstract pieces covered every inch of available wall space. There was joy in them, there was love and happiness, and there was pain, suffering, and darkness that could only be described as death.

A chill ran through him. It was as if he were seeing bits and pieces of his own life put on display and it was unsettling. He was certain that Lexi had done the paintings herself and it had him questioning just what horrors she'd been through in her life to bring out such a raw and emotional response.

He heard her as her bare feet softly padded back into the room and he turned to face her. "I'm sure you're tired. There's a spare bedroom upstairs - last door on your left. The bathroom is the first door on the left."

"Yeah, I have to admit that I'm kind of feeling the wreck." He walked to the stairs and placed his hand on the glossy oak banister. "You're a very trusting woman, Lexi. I may look menacing, but for what it's worth, I promise you that you have nothing to fear from me. I'm thankful and grateful for your hospitality."

"I'm not worried." She grinned at him as she continued. "My daddy taught me to shoot, and I have no qualms about pulling a trigger if I have to. Goodnight, Blaze."

He started up the stairs but paused to look back and saw her turn and walk to one of the bookshelves, pick a book at random and curl up in a large chair. Definitely something there, he thought. Something bad. Something that had left her in a world of hurt.

He understood exactly how she felt.

Sitting on the side of the queen-sized bed, Blaze took a moment to evaluate and process the predicament he'd fallen into. He looked around the cozy room and breathed his first easy breath since he'd woken on her couch. Exquisite woman - unusual situation, he mused. Major snowstorm, fucked up car – but at least there was a roof over his head, and he had a soft bed in a warm house. He'd slept in far less pleasant accommodations in his lifetime. And though they were in an odd situation, he was grateful for her kindness.

He couldn't believe the optimistic view he'd had when the day had started had gotten him stuck in a blizzard with a wrecked car, dependent on the generosity of a stranger. Oh! And he probably had a concussion, which was just exactly what he needed. Something else to mess with the fucked up workings of his brain. "Well, I'll just have to make the most of it," he muttered to himself and began stripping out of his clothes.

He stretched out his muscles, tensed and aching from the wreck, then crawled naked beneath the covers. His body, long used to sleeping in unfamiliar surroundings, relaxed into the soft mattress with a sigh of relief. His mind, trained to turn off and sleep on command, immediately took him under.

It wasn't until a couple of hours later that his subconscious took him down the rough and rocky path into the recurring nightmare that had a stranglehold on his life.

Chapter Three

Lexi wasn't exactly sure what to make of him. He seemed nice enough, but his first reaction upon waking had startled her more than she cared to admit. His fighting stance led her to believe that he was well trained in hand-to-hand combat and had probably used those lethal skills more than a few times.

But while there was a hardness to his exterior, there was something softer underneath. Something searching, seeking. Yes, she thought, there was definitely something more to the man currently occupying her guest room.

As she'd sat with him while he'd eaten, she'd looked into his chocolate brown eyes and seen more than she'd wanted to. She'd always had empathic abilities, blessing and curse, and sensing the pain he tried to hide made her hurt for him. Taking a deep breath, she chastised herself and promised not to get involved. He would be with her for a couple of days and then be out of her life. Simple as that.

Still, she thought, he was certainly a pleasure to look at. He'd shaved his head at some point and the shadow of stubble was just beginning to show through. And while there was no hair to speak of on his head, a week's worth of facial hair sat neatly and perfectly groomed on his handsome face causing her to wonder if he intended to grow it out further. Strong cheekbones pulled the eye to a set of plump, kissable lips and she found herself wondering if his kisses would be tender or strong, or some crazy combination of the two.

Lexi stopped herself. Obviously, she'd been without sex way too damn long to be having thoughts of kissing a complete stranger. Time to change directions, she thought, and get off that path before she wandered too far down it.

She returned the book she'd only halfway been reading to the shelf and began going through her nightly routine, banking the fire and turning off lights before she climbed the stairs. She entered her bedroom and began to undress before she suddenly remembered her guest and closed and locked the door. She was a trusting soul, but not that trusting.

Once she'd slipped on her long t-shirt, she walked over to the window and leaned against the sill. The storm raged on, and Lexi found that the fierceness outside somehow helped to settle her restlessness.

There was just something calming to her about knowing she wasn't alone in her misery, that the elements recognized her struggles and in a strange way, offered their sympathy, partnering with her as her anguish and grief raged on in an internal battle. And even more calming to her was knowing that the storm would eventually back off and stop altogether. She just hoped that one day she'd be able to find her own inner peace and escape at last from her personal storm.

The tiredness she felt from the storm preparations called her to bed and she snuggled in and stared up at the skylight overhead. It was pitch black now, completely covered with snow, but normally she could look up, see the stars and make a few wishes. And those wishes, her most fervent, were that she'd been able to live the life she'd envisioned on that riverbank all those years ago. Those wishes would never change, but that wouldn't stop her from making them.

With thoughts of what her life should have been floating through her mind, she drifted off to sleep.

Loud moans, sounds of anguish, a distressed animal crying out in pain, echoed through the house and startled Lexi from sleep. Her heart pounded, her breath caught, and she found herself listening closely, unsure of exactly what she was hearing. The sounds of a soul being tortured carried once again through the normally silent house and echoed in her ears. Lexi jumped out of bed and quickly hurried down the hall.

When she got to her guest room, she wasn't sure what to do. Should she barge in? Was it safe? She couldn't take the hurt and pain she heard coming from Blaze who was obviously caught in a nightmare.

She knocked on the closed door, but the horror continued. She knocked again, beating harder against the solid wood, and still the terror raged on. She tried the doorknob, and finding it unlocked, eased inside the room.

The dim light that relieved the total darkness of the bedroom revealed that Blaze was in bed, his body tensed and his hands gripping the sheets as his head whipped back and forth while the horror of the dream ripped through him. His body jerked and once again he cried out in pain.

He had to wake up, but she wasn't sure how to make that happen. She'd read about night terrors, had been known to experience more than a few herself, but wasn't certain how to pull him from the abyss.

She flipped the switch on a lamp that gave soft light to the room, then stood at the end of the bed, her arms crossed over her chest, fear in her eyes, and called to him.

"Blaze. Come on, Blaze. Wake up. You're safe. I promise you're safe here. Please, please wake up!"

Nothing. She tried again and again until eventually she broke through the hell he was reliving.

Once more his training kicked in, deep in the recesses of his mind, and had him startling awake. He quickly sat up, the sheet he'd used falling to his waist and revealing his broad naked chest, a solid mural of vibrant tattoos.

Her breath caught as she realized just how beautiful the man before her was. Even as he struggled to get awake and aware, the sexual vibes he threw off had her mouth-watering and heat tingling through her body. It was a strange sensation, one that she hadn't experienced since before Jackson had died.

She continued talking to him, hoping she could finish pulling him out of the nightmare.

"Blaze. You're safe. Do you know where you're at? West Virginia, in the mountains. Remember me? Lexi? You're in my house."

He gently shook his head back and forth trying to clear out the dregs of the memories that haunted and chased him, and suddenly it all came flooding back to him. His body relaxed, his vision cleared, and he saw Lexi standing before him.

"Yeah. Sorry. I'm okay. Did I scare you? God, I'm so sorry."

"It's okay, really." She relaxed her posture, her arms falling to her sides in relief. "I'm sorry I barged in, but I had to try to wake you."

"Thanks."

"I'll just…" she gestured out the door and took a few steps backward before she turned to go. Then with a final look back at his gorgeous face and magnificent body, she closed the door and rushed to her room. When she was safe inside, the door locked, she leaned against it and let the shaking begin.

This was the first time she'd been on this side of the nightmare. With a wave of regret she realized just how terrifying it must have been for her mother as she'd comforted and soothed her through the gamut of emotions that Lexi had experienced when she'd first mourned Jackson, buried in grief and despair.

When the shaking finally stopped, when she felt more in control, she walked to the bathroom that adjoined her bedroom and downed a full glass of water, easing her dry throat. Then she splashed cool water on her face, took a deep breath, and crawled back under the covers.

It was a long time before she drifted off again, and as she lay there, she wondered what horrendous trauma he must have endured to be so haunted in his dreams.

Because there was no doubt in her mind, with what she'd just experienced with him, he was definitely dealing with his own PTSD.

Blaze had watched her leave, a scared rabbit anxious to get away. He couldn't blame her. He wished it was as easy for him to escape his nightmares. He'd started having them about a year before, occasional and rare at first, then happening more and more often, to the point that they were almost nightly. When they'd picked up in frequency, he'd known he was going to have to make a change. But it had taken him a long time to realize that the change he'd needed to make, the change that was mandatory for his survival, was to walk away, to escape the life he'd been living.

After he felt he'd given her enough time to have fallen back asleep, he slipped on his jeans, eased out of the guest room and into the bathroom down the hall. He splashed cold water on his face and stared at himself in the mirror. He knew, somehow, some way, he was going to have to find the ability to let his past go, to put it behind him and move on. He just wasn't sure how to begin the process.

He supposed the most logical thing to do was to see about therapy. But he knew there were things he'd done and seen that he hoped he would never have to revisit, not while he was awake and aware. Things he hoped each and every night he wouldn't have to see in his dreams, though they appeared time and again.

Time. Right now, he thought, he just wanted time, he needed space, some distance from his trauma. With any luck and by some small miracle, maybe time would help him start to heal.

He found himself wide awake and restless, a perpetual state of late it seemed. He wandered back downstairs, the plush carpet cushioning his steps and keeping his movements quiet. When he reached the living room he looked back over at the wall of paintings as the soft glow from the fire danced with shadows and light, and again he wondered about the woman upstairs. Pain recognized pain, he thought.

Walking to the bookcase he chose a Grisham and stretched out in the same chair Lexi had earlier in the evening. Reading calmed his mind, helped him escape, and before the end of the first chapter, he was fast asleep with the book sprawled open on his bare chest.

Dawn came early and though Lexi would have preferred to stay in bed, there were chores to do. A strict routine had gone a long way toward keeping her from falling off the emotional cliff she balanced upon on a daily basis.

She dressed, adding an extra layer due to the snow and cold, and grabbed her waterproof boots and heavy outerwear. Quietly slipping past Blaze sleeping deeply and awkwardly in the chair, she was out the door before the sun had barely risen, shoveling a path from the deck around to the goat pen.

After feeding and making sure their water wasn't frozen, and the heat lamp in their shelter was working, she shoveled over to the chicken house and continued the process. She tried to make as few trips to town as she could and after a couple of winters being without basics during major storms such as this one, she'd made the decision to always have milk and eggs on hand, at the very least. Goat's milk may not have been her first choice or what she'd been used to, but it had grown on her, and she loved caring for her animals.

She gathered the eggs her hens had laid, placing them carefully in her basket, then went back to the goats to do their milking. By the time she was done she was half frozen, but she knew it would be worth the effort to have everything cleared out and ready for a repeat process later that evening.

She had just climbed the deck stairs and was stomping the snow from her boots when the front door opened, startling her. She wasn't sure how she kept ahold of her bucket and basket, but she did so and only let out a small squeal of surprise at Blaze as he stood scowling at her.

"What the hell are you doing? Do you want to get frostbite?"

"Damn it! You just cost me two lives. What does it look like I'm doing?" He held the door for her and once she was inside, took the spoils of her labor from her so she could remove her heavy gear and boots.

"What is all this?"

"Obviously, those are eggs and that is milk. I would have thought you would have heard of them by now."

"Quite the smartass, aren't you? I meant, why are you walking around with eggs and milk when there's a foot of snow on the damn ground?"

Hands on hips she met him eye to eye, indignant that he would question her actions. "The goats needed tending and milking, and the chickens needed caring for as well, and as I was already out there, it made sense to gather the eggs. I do it daily. Plus, the snow needed shoveling. I went ahead and did it so that I wouldn't have to go back out and do it later."

"You raise your own chickens and drink goat's milk?"

"Yes, I do. Is there something wrong with that?"

"No. I guess I just didn't expect it."

"Just what did you expect?"

"I, well...I don't suppose I had thought about it. I guess, with conditions like this popping up with only a moment's notice, it would be beneficial. So, what can I do to help?"

"You can take those into the kitchen. I'll be in to take care of them in a minute."

She continued stripping out of her heavy coat, hanging it on a pretty rack by the door, and taking her hat, gloves and scarf, laid them on the hearth to dry. He'd built the fire back up while she'd been out and for that she was grateful.

She stood for a moment warming herself by the fire, letting the feeling return to her fingers and toes, tingling sensations letting her know her frozen blood was once again circulating freely throughout her body.

She turned her back to the fire and found him standing on the other side of the couch watching her as she let the heat continue to warm her.

"Since I'm stuck here, how about you tell me what I can do to make up for your hospitality? I'm not much help in the kitchen as far as cooking, but I can chop vegetables or wash dishes, maybe help with the animals. I do actually have some winter clothes in the truck if I can make it down there. I don't want you to feel like you have to wait on me."

"I appreciate that, but I'm used to doing things for myself. I can take you down in the Gator after breakfast. It'll make it." She rolled her eyes, "Probably." She made her way into the kitchen and went about storing the milk and eggs. With every move she made she felt his eyes on her and it unnerved her. "How's your head?"

"Better. It still hurts like a son-of-a-bitch, but it's better. And, hey, I'm only seeing one of you now and not two."

Concern laced its way through her voice as she turned to look at him. "You were seeing double?"

"Yeah, things were a little messed up there for a bit. I had a few memories come back to me overnight. When you pulled me from the truck, I thought you were an angel. Then, with the double vision, I thought there were two angels and that I was finally dead." He started to say more but stopped himself, the animation that had been on his face disappearing as quickly as it had appeared.

Unsure of what to say, Lexi decided avoidance was the best path. "Why don't you go relax in the living room? I'll have some breakfast ready soon." At that moment, his stomach growled loudly causing Lexi to laugh. "Maybe I better make some extra."

Her laugh sent chills down his spine. It was beautiful, melodic, and he found himself hoping to hear it again. He ran a hand over his smooth head and looked anywhere in the kitchen he could as long as it wasn't at her. His line of sight landed on a coffee maker. "Coffee. I can make coffee."

"If it will make you feel better, then fine. Go for it." She smiled an easy smile at him. "Coffee and filters are in the cabinet above the coffee maker, cups too."

They went to work, each with their own agenda and within moments the smells of bacon frying, and freshly brewed coffee scented the air. She quickly had breakfast put together and on the small kitchen table that sat against a wide, arching panel of windows. Blaze carried two steaming mugs to the table and stood staring out at the picture-perfect scene on the other side of the glass, pensive, lost in his thoughts.

"It makes for quite the view, doesn't it?"

She'd taken him off guard with her question, having almost forgotten she was anywhere around, and his mind returned slowly from the path it had wandered down. "Yes, it really does. I want something just like this. I want to be able to look out on that kind of view every day for the rest of my life."

"Well, I hope you find what you're looking for, the land and view. How long have you been looking?"

"I'm just starting, actually." He offered a crooked smile. "Yesterday was the maiden voyage for my mission."

"Well, that was some voyage. It took me a while to find this, a while longer to build the house."

"You built this?"

"Yeah. I wanted something that was mine, only mine. I wanted my ideas and my ideas alone, laid out how I wanted them, in a manner that works for me. I didn't want to go into an existing house and remodel it. I don't think I ever would have been happy taking someone else's ideas and changing it to fit my needs. I don't think I ever could have gotten exactly what I wanted if I hadn't started from the beginning and designed it from the ground up."

"It's beautiful. Functional. It flows nicely, room to room. I don't know you, but I'd say it suits you."

"Thanks."

They fell into silence once again as they ate, and when she was done, she sat back and looked at him over the rim of her mug as she savored her coffee, watching as he continued to devour what remained of the full plate of food before him.

"I don't want to intrude, Blaze, but...last night. Does that happen often?"

He paused mid-chew and stared down at his plate, his voracious appetite suddenly disappearing. He finished the bite he was working on and swallowed slowly as he began absently pushing the remaining food on his plate back and forth with his fork.

"Lately it's a nightly occurrence. I'm sorry. If I could stop it, could control it, I'd never have scared you that way."

"Have you talked to anyone about it?"

He shook his head and carefully laid the fork on his plate. "I can't - not yet, anyway." He stood and picked up their plates. "You cooked; I'll wash."

"Alright." Well, she thought, case closed and subject dropped. She understood the feeling, respected it, and was unoffended. She finished her coffee and carried her cup to the sink where he stood running hot soapy water. Then she turned and left him to seek out solitude for herself.

Chapter Four

She escaped to her studio, seeking the solace and comfort she always found there. She'd taken the large room and outfitted it with everything she would ever need to work on her music in hopes that one day she would hear it, feel it again, but the music had never returned. The equipment, the piano, the stacks of blank staff paper, waited, always ready for her in the hope that she would someday push past her mental block.

When she'd first gotten settled in her home she'd written, needing an outlet for her creativity. She still wrote, putting her thoughts into poetry, snippets of memories, sharing her thoughts with only herself. And over the past couple of years, she'd taken a corner of the room and turned it into an artist's corner. A large easel sat near a wall of floor-to-ceiling windows with a canvas, painting partially finished, waiting for her to pour her heart into it, to finish it off.

That was where she headed, her inner turmoil rushing to the surface, feeling as if this stranger had somehow churned the ever-battering tide inside, the waves of empathy smothering her, drowning in the pain she knew he tried to hide. She had to release the whirlpool of emotion he'd stirred before she simply went under and never re-surfaced.

So, she painted, each stroke blending, slashing, highlighting, shadows and light, a riot of colors, until at last she felt calm again. Heart beating rapidly, she took a step back and stared at the finished canvas. Tears streaked her face, tears that had no choice but to fall with an outpouring of emotion from the depths of her soul, and as she swiped absently at the liquid trail of emotion, she took a stuttering breath.

"You are luminous, so beautiful. I could watch you do that, paint like that, for hours." He'd startled her again, and she whirled on him, alarm quickly turning to anger at the intrusion.

"What are you doing? What the hell are you doing in here?" Daggers shot from her eyes with the demanding questions.

He held up his hands in defense. "Sorry. I didn't mean to interrupt. I knocked but you were...lost. Lost in your work and there was this," he waved a hand in a downward motion in front of his face, "veil. I knocked, I spoke to you, but there was no getting through."

She eased her stance, tamped down the anger, and composed herself. "No. I'm sorry. I shouldn't have gone at you like that. I just wasn't expecting you to be there."

"You've been at this for a while. I just thought, if you don't mind, I'll take your ATV down to get my stuff." She checked the time and was shocked to see how late it was getting.

"I didn't realize what time it was. I'll take you now, then I'll see to the animals while you get settled."

"Ok. I appreciate it."

The Gator handled the snow without problem, making it to his truck in only a few minutes. He quickly grabbed his heavy coat from the back seat and slipped it on. He took a moment to check out the damage to the truck, and with a muttered curse, grabbed his duffle bag out of the back and climbed back in the ATV.

Lexi looked at him curiously. "Is that everything?"

He looked down at the duffle, back to her, and with a nod in the affirmative, settled back for the return ride up to the house.

Lexi parked the Gator and began her trek over to the goats and chickens. She'd just finished putting out more feed when she looked up to see him walking toward her.

"What can I do to help?"

"Nothing. I've got it."

"Are you always this damn stubborn?"

"Absolutely."

"Just tell me something I can help with. It's the least I can do to repay you for letting me stay."

"You don't owe me anything, but fine. The hens need checking to see if there are more eggs."

"Hens. Eggs. Ok, yeah. I can do that."

She grinned as she watched him figure out the gate to the hen house and maneuver his large body inside. When the hens started to fuss and he came rushing out, she had to laugh. "Something wrong?"

"You have attack chickens. A little warning would have been nice." When she began laughing harder, the scowl on his face quickly shifted and soon he was laughing with her. "Okay. You got me. Maybe you can show me what needs doing, how to do it? I really do want to help and," he looked around at the snow-covered mountain, "I figure that if I'm going have my own place, this kind of setup might not be a bad idea."

"Yeah. I can do that." She walked him through her thought process with the animals as they tended, showed him where everything was, talked to him about their needs and how to go about caring for them and maintaining their environment.

When he successfully retrieved his first egg, excitement lit his eyes and his crooked grin appeared. It was then that the first fluttering of desire raced through her body, stirring feelings she'd thought she'd buried with Jackson, feelings she'd never thought to have again.

Panic fluttered throughout her body, and she turned, escaping to the house to hide in her sanctuary.

Lexi gave him the number for a towing service, and as Blaze made the call, she went upstairs to her bathroom. Her muscles ached from shoveling snow that morning and she desperately wanted a soak in her tub.

The bathroom she'd designed was large, a luxury indulgence she had given herself without a moment of guilt. A full-size walk-in shower sat in one corner enclosed with a block glass wall, while a garden tub sat beneath a wide window, sunk in the floor with a stone ledge surrounding it, facing a small stone fireplace. Dark granite flooring was offset by warm apricot-colored walls, and crystal globes surrounded drop lighting strategically placed throughout the room.

She lit the fire while the bath was running and added salts to help ease her aches and pains. She pinned her hair up, a mass of auburn curls perched on top of her head, and when she settled in the tub her body sighed with relief.

She closed her eyes, rested her neck on a fluffy towel pillowing her head on the edge of the tub, and drifted. And as she drifted her mind wandered, going back over her life, those highs and lows that she never really escaped from, and it wasn't long until she nodded off, exhaustion taking her under quickly.

Her nightmares had lessened over the years and were fewer and further between, but when they hit, they hit hard. Flashes of her life looped through her mind. Then the memories mixed, reality and fiction converging, separating, and converging once again. They made for a footage reel that didn't exist, until at last, images of both wrecks, the one with Jackson and the one with Blaze, dominated her dream. Still shot after still shot haunted her and caused her to scream, her mind and body thrashing in agony as each image forcefully careened through her unconsciousness.

When the screams came, blood-curdling and deafening, Blaze, terrified at what could have happened, raced up the stairs and pounded his fist on her bedroom door. The screaming continued and he tried the knob.

Frustrated and panicked at finding it locked and seeing no other way to help her, he simply burst through the door. Wood splintered as the latch ripped from the frame and the door tore from its hinges. And still the screams continued, agonizing terror wrenching at his soul. He didn't see her but saw what he assumed was the bathroom, door open, and he rushed inside.

When he realized she was in the tub, that she was having a nightmare, he ran to her and swiftly yanked her from the water that had gone tepid, wrapping her in a tight embrace, knowing that when his own past chased him, the one thing he wanted more than anything was to have someone to hold onto, to comfort him in his misery.

She came awake suddenly and just as quickly realized he held her, naked and dripping wet against him, softly speaking soothing words to her. And while he soothed, he reached for the towel by the tub and bundled it around her still trembling body.

"It's okay. I've got you. Just hold on to me."

Still shaken and confused by the dream, she didn't have the strength to argue. She simply laid her head against his shoulder and let the tears fall silently. Comfort, though it was in the arms of a stranger, was more welcome than she could have thought possible.

When the tears finally slowed and then stopped, she slowly stepped away from him, securing the towel more tightly around herself.

"Thank you, Blaze."

His hand reached out and he wiped gently at the trail of tears on her face. "I won't ask if you're alright, because I know how it is. I won't apologize for pulling you from whatever trauma chases you. But I will apologize for the damage to your bedroom door. It was the only way I could get to you. And with the way you were screaming, I had no other choice. I had to check, had to make sure."

Once again, he ran his hand over his head, looked up at the ceiling, and finding nothing else to say, looked her in the eyes, nodded once, and walked out, leaving her standing there staring after him.

She heard him as he picked up the door, leaned it against the wall. Then she heard the quiet click of the guest room door as he closed himself inside.

She dressed and then made her way downstairs. Shaken, she'd taken some time after he'd left to gather herself, to get her head on straight. To go back through the dream and break it apart, piece by piece, so that she could separate what was real, and what wasn't. By the time she'd done that she'd realized she was starving, and that she was ready for dinner.

She supposed that she owed Blaze an explanation after she'd likely taken a few years off his life. After all, she'd just subjected him to her own personal horror.

Unfortunately, with all she'd been through, she did not easily trust. And while he'd certainly not given her any reason to distrust him, sharing such intimacies with him while she was naked and shaking in the middle of her bathroom hadn't seemed to be the appropriate time nor place.

She pulled out pots and pans, the ingredients she needed, and got to work. By the time Blaze appeared in the kitchen the air was scented with the aroma of spicy tomato sauce and Lexi was draining the water from a pot of pasta.

Saying nothing, Blaze went to the cabinet and retrieved plates and utensils, and went about setting the table. Lexi set the steaming bowl of spaghetti between them, a platter with garlic toast, and soon they were seated and eating their dinner, uncomfortable silence echoing around them.

When Lexi stopped eating and looked up at him, he paused, waiting to see what she would say. He assumed she was going to lay into him, berate him and tell him that he should have minded his own business, demand he fix her door, and stay away from her. What he didn't expect was for her to begin to tell him about the dream and the reasons why she was plagued by the same nightmare over and over.

Halfway through her story he found himself reaching a hand across the table to her to offer sympathy, comfort, and understanding. He hadn't expected her to take his offered hand but was pleased when she did, and he enclosed it in both of his, taking a breath before he spoke.

"I don't know where to begin to tell you how sorry I am. You were dealt a bad hand, Lexi."

"I've come to terms with it, mostly. I'm not as numb as I used to be. After Jackson, and then my parents, when the numbness set in, I had to get away, to start over, to find...something. What I found was my mountain top. I had to build a new life, and in building my new life, I built this."

She gestured around her home, out the window to the snowy landscape. "I'm not telling you this for your sympathy, but simply to let you know that I understand. You don't have to tell me your story, but I want you to know you aren't alone in this harsh world we live in."

She slid her hand out of his and went back to eating, silence reigning once again.

With dinner cleared and the dishes done, they settled into the living room, Lexi in a chair, Blaze on the couch.

"Can I ask a question?"

She looked at him and smiled, "You can ask. It depends on the question as to whether I will answer or not." A teasing light twinkled in her eyes and had him chuckling softly.

"Oh, it isn't a difficult question. At least I don't think so. Unless I've missed it, I haven't seen a TV. Actually, the only electronic things like that I've seen were in your studio, and while you obviously keep a neat house, there was definitely a layer of dust on your recording equipment, the piano and such. Why is that?"

The light in her eyes dimmed some. "I guess I didn't tell you that part of the story."

He held up his hands to stop her, not wanting to upset her any more than she'd already been that evening. "I'm sorry. I shouldn't have asked."

"No. It's alright." She paused. "At one point in my life, I sang. Music was a huge part of me, my life, and what I wanted for my future. I even had a record deal, went on tour. But all of that was before Jackson died. Something broke in me that day and I tried for several months after, to fix it, to stitch it back together and get on with my life.

"Then my parents died, and I was never able to mend myself. At least not that part of me. I had hoped when I built this place, when I escaped, that one day the music would return, that I would be able to feel again the way I'd always felt when I let the music take control. After all this time? I've decided it may never come back.

"I do have a laptop, but I rarely use it. I keep up with a handful of lifelong friends by email. I use it for supplies, for weather updates, and on very rare occasions I check to see what is going on in the world. No TV. No radio. I find that I need the quiet and have no need to fill the silence. I have my books, my art. I try to live simply, and simply live. I really don't need more than that. At least not at this point in my life."

He'd listened as she'd explained, digesting all she'd said. Feeling and understanding the pain in her words. "Okay. I can see that."

Silence fell again. Lexi walked into the kitchen and was opening a bottle of wine when she sensed he'd joined her. She pulled two long-stemmed wine glasses from a cabinet, poured and offered one to him.

He stood leaning against the counter, legs and arms crossed before him, glass in hand. He started to speak but stopped, sipped, and paused again. Then he downed the wine and emptied the glass. He blew out a breath of resignation, then began telling his own story.

"I was in the Navy. I did my time and then some. I received commendations and special acknowledgments for a job well done, moved up the ranks and moved up quickly, and kind of figured that I'd be in for life. When my last re-enlistment was up, I was encouraged to join a special forces unit. At that point, it all seemed like some huge adventure, an opportunity to continue with what I knew, but something different at the same time.

"All I'd ever known was the service as I'd joined straight out of high school, so I did it, me and one of my closest friends. Now, I wonder if it was the biggest mistake of my life. I can't give you many details because it's all classified, but I did things, saw things…I will live with those horrors for the rest of my life. It was a whirlwind of travel, rushing from place to place, doing our job, and then moving on to the next spot in the blink of an eye." He paused and closed his eyes once more before continuing.

"We were supposed to be there to help keep peace, to help the oppressed, abused, mistreated, and we did. But what we had to do to get them out, to get them safe, to remove the oppressors? It got to be more than my conscience could take." He opened his eyes once more and looked deeply into hers.

"I was already thinking about getting out and more than ready to leave that life behind when I lost my friend. Sniper took him out. I watched my friend die. Watched the life drain right out of him while I held him, his blood pouring from the wound, coating my hands. It was my fault, you see, but he didn't blame me. His last words to me were how proud he was to have served with me. But it was my fault." Despair and rage, true anger at himself rang in his words. "I was to have been his backup. But I left him."

She walked to him with the wine, refilled his glass, and waited. "A kid, she couldn't have been more than three or four years old, so a baby, really, wandered from one of the houses right into the line of fire. I yelled for her to go back, to go find her parents, to hide, but she just stood there, tears running down her dirt-smeared face, clutching a ragged little doll against her. I couldn't...damn it! She was so tiny, helpless. I had to get her out of there, I had to get her to safety. And in doing so, in saving her life, I let my friend die. His blood is on my hands, and I don't think I'll ever look at them," he set his glass down and held his hands in front of himself, staring as if they were foreign objects, "and not see red. I see his blood and I feel like I'll never be clean."

She placed her hand on his arm and offered comfort. "Blaze. You did what you had to do."

"I know that. Deep down I know that. My friend lost his life to save another, and I know that's how he would have wanted it, but it haunts me. All of it haunts me. The blood, the gore, the senseless loss of life. I joined the Navy to make a difference. Every day, every night when the nightmares hit, I question if anything I did, even one tiny thing, made any kind of difference."

"I'd say you made a difference, Blaze. Especially for one little girl."

He inhaled deeply, then straightened and took another sip of wine before setting his glass on the counter again. Then he did what he'd wanted to do from the first moment he'd laid his eyes on her.

The assault on her mouth was intense, a fevered rush of lips, tongue and teeth - licking, nipping, devouring. When he felt her body simply begin to melt against his, to surrender to desires she'd so long denied, his hands began to roam. Her body felt amazing to him, feminine and soft, but with a steel core underneath that aroused him even further. And when the moan came, pleasure mingled with desire - from her? From him? Both? Something snapped inside him, and he jerked back, his lungs burning, breathless with need. He quickly stepped away.

"I'm sorry. Dear God, I'm sorry. I shouldn't have." He straightened, and seeing the dazed look in her eyes, turned and left her standing there, aroused and confused.

He'd gone straight to bed. She sat in the living room trying to read but couldn't get her mind off the kiss. He'd left her standing there, lost in the onslaught of feelings he'd unearthed, cravings she'd long thought buried, forgotten, and no longer needed or wanted. Part of her was glad, extremely glad he hadn't continued, that he'd pulled back. But there was another part, and it kept rearing its ugly head every few minutes, that had desperately wanted more, had yearned to feel his touch, to feel anything and everything, once again.

She berated herself over and over, told herself to not get involved, to be glad that he would be leaving soon. But the kiss had unlocked a long-denied hunger inside her and was making her stir crazy. She'd sat, she'd paced, she'd sat again, and eventually, she'd found herself back in her studio, staring at the piano, wishing with all her being that another kind of spark would ignite inside herself. With shaking hands, her fingers lightly touched the keys, longing for that part of herself that had been extinguished so many years ago.

But the music didn't come. What had once flowed from her without thought didn't offer her a trickle of hope. Defeated and frustrated, she stomped up the stairs and readied herself for bed.

He couldn't believe he'd lost control like that. This beautiful, amazing woman had been kind enough to share her home with him, temporary though it was, and he'd all but ravished her in her pretty and tidy little kitchen. Now he paced in his room, unaware that she'd done the same downstairs, their movements mimicking each other as they tried to figure out what they were feeling and whether to act on it or not.

From the first glimpse he'd had of her, he'd wanted her, and in the short time they'd been together that lust had quickly turned to a burning need. And while they were still strangers, he felt he was getting to know her quickly, the result of forced togetherness. His heart, already broken over the loss of his friend, torn and struggling daily with the knowledge of his past, had simply been ripped to pieces, shredded, when she'd told him of her fiancé, her parents.

She'd endured more than one person should ever have to face and she'd come through the other side. She was still broken, still healing, but she'd made it through. He only hoped he could find half the strength she'd shown so that he could find his way through the darkness that threatened to eclipse his life. Somehow, some way, he had to face the obstacles in his path and come out the other side.

When she'd shared her background, the loss of her music, he'd wanted to hold her, simply hold her, until one of them had regained their footing. Instead, he'd opened up about his own past and once he'd poured his heart out, swamped with emotion, he'd had no choice. His thoughts and feelings had been all over the place, his soul bared. And with all that he'd buried deep suddenly brought to the surface, he'd found himself overwhelmed with desire for her. He'd had such a need to taste her, to feel her, to have her staunch the bleeding from the open wounds that desecrated his soul.

He wasn't sure what had happened, what had brought him to his senses, but escape had been his only thought as he'd left her standing there, so soft, so willing, so tempting. He could have had her, knew she would have given in, and the knowledge that he could have, would have, taken advantage of her that way rent yet another piece of him, leaving him hollowed out.

When he finally slept, he was even more restless than usual and he knew the nightmare lurking in the recesses of his mind, would be coming for him and coming harder and faster than normal. All he could do was hang on by his fingernails and pray that it would be over quickly.

Chapter Five

They'd been there for three long days. Sweltering heat had their uniforms clinging to their bodies, trapping even more heat and humidity against their skin. The Commander's order to hold steady was always one that caused his anxiety to heighten, but over the years he'd gotten used to it, and had learned to use that spike to his advantage. It was still hard to do though when he was on pins and needles, ready to take action.

The village, nothing more than a small, cleared-out space in the jungle, a smattering of thatched roofs barely visible through the encroaching wildness that surrounded it. Dirt paths now turned to mud thanks to recent heavy rains, circled and looped, only wide enough for foot traffic, or for the "wealthy" of the village, a bicycle.

It was time. Orders to move had finally come down the pipe and Blaze was more than ready. This was it – his last mission before he could go home. He was ready and had already put in his papers. He had to get out. He had to get home.

West Virginia.

A calling from deep in his soul had him restless and yearning to get back and he couldn't wait to see those beautiful mountains again. He'd sworn he'd make it back and he was determined that once he did, he would find a place and make it his own.

He was ready to leave the constant upheaval of this life and at long last put his past behind him, to find peace within his soul.

The signal came and he and his men were immediately thrown into action. Shots rang out and the enemy made their presence known. For what seemed like hours bullets pinged off houses, off trees, and when they found their target, they ripped through flesh, muscle, and bone.

Movement caught his eye as tiny feet caked in mud ran from one of the huts. Eyes wild and scared, the toddler stood, thumb in mouth, a homemade baby doll held tightly against the dirty, ragged material that made up her baggy, shapeless dress.

Blaze looked toward the hut she'd run from and saw no movement. Where were her parents? Why didn't they get her? His heart thrummed in fear for the child. She needed help or she was going to die. He couldn't let that happen.

A lightning bolt of speed, he rushed from cover into the madness that raged through the village. He reached her quickly, scooped her into his arms, and just as quickly, got the hell out of the line of fire. He knew he'd taken a chance, but she was so innocent, a baby. She didn't deserve all that was happening around her and he could not, would not, see her lose her life.

He got her back to the hut she'd run from and through the ramshackle door to find the only other person in the hovel was her mother – deeply in the throes of hard labor with the toddler's baby brother or sister. Panic set in. He wasn't trained for this. He didn't have to worry but for a moment, though, as in the few minutes he was debating what to do, the baby was born and began its newborn cry.

Was the baby crying so hard, so loud, because it had been evicted from the comfort and safety of its home only to be born into the madness of a warzone? Thoughts whirled and screamed inside his head as he tried to make sense of the atrocity of war and the unfathomable damage that it always left behind.

The mother, long practiced and sure in her movements, cared for the baby and herself, and as she did so she urged him to go. Her personal crisis had passed and with the newborn at her breast and her toddler curled next to her, she was content and at peace though the madness raged on outside her tiny world.

He left, quickly returning to his post to get himself back on track with his duties. Before he could make it there, more enemy fire rang out. He'd been shot before, knew what it felt like, and when he heard the sounds of the guns and saw the ricochet of bullets as they pinged nearby, he waited to feel the sting of his skin being pierced. But it didn't come. This time, the bullets missed his body as he ran at full speed for cover, and instead found a more stationary target. Seeing his comrade, his friend, take a bullet that was intended for himself broke something inside him, something he was afraid would never, could never heal.

He knew as he reached him that he would be losing his friend. The shot had blood pouring from the wound, a gushing river of red that could not be stopped. Pain-filled eyes looked up at him with understanding. His friend knew the lengths he'd gone to for the child, knew what it had cost Blaze to make that decision, and knew, without a doubt, that his time on earth was done.

Blood on his hands, on his uniform, and on his soul, he threw his head back and screamed his rage at the unfairness of losing one life to save another.

She'd been asleep for a couple of hours when the unmistakable and agonizing sounds of horrendous pain pierced the still, silent night once again. She didn't think, just reacted. She ran to his room, calling to him, calling for him, hoping she could break through the dream once again, and coax him back to reality.

Scared but taking a chance, she sat on the side of the bed and gently placed her hand on his broad chest while she spoke to him, soothed him, and calmed him. When he came to this time, he emerged from a fog, his mind, his eyes, his senses slowly clearing the mists of the dream as the room came into focus and he became aware of his surroundings.

He grabbed her hand and held it close to his chest as he sat up, savoring the warmth of her touch. With his other hand he reached for her, cradling her cheek in his palm and staring into her concerned eyes. When he lightly brushed his thumb across her lips, relishing their softness, she surprised him by kissing the pad tentatively.

Arousal shot straight to his groin, and the low growl that escaped his lips had her instantly dripping with desire, liquid warmth flooding her, making her want, making her need.

"Lexi," he whispered, and she went willingly into his arms. He lay back on the bed, pulling her down on top of him as he kissed her, "damn it. We shouldn't be doing this, Angel." But his kisses never stopped. More, he wanted more, had to have more. He had such hunger, such thirst, and she was the only sustenance that would give him relief and quench the flames that burned within.

"Yes, yes we should."

He moved down to her throat, wanting to taste her there, to feel the beat of her heart as her blood thrummed rapidly through her veins. "I don't want to hurt you."

"You won't, Blaze. You won't. I need this, too."

Their lips met again, and their hunger reached new levels. She felt the steel of his cock beneath the thin sheet that covered him, and it made her ache to feel him inside. She straddled him, then sat up to remove her long sleep shirt.

He watched as her body was revealed to him, slender but curvy. He ran his hands from her hips to her waist and back again as she looked down at him, memorizing the feel of her, sinewy muscle hidden underneath her soft, supple skin. And when he smoothed them back up her body to cup her breasts, the hunger that had been waiting patiently to be fed, took control.

He sat up and wrapped her in his arms as his mouth feasted, licking one taught nipple then the other before sucking it in and teasing it with his tongue, the soft pulls sending dizzying sensations throughout her body.

She let her head fall back as she reveled in the attention he gave her, and her hands, never still, traced a course of their own, her fingers massaging each hard muscle they discovered as he made her burn. When he ripped her lacy thong from her body, she gasped his name.

The scent of her arousal made his already aching cock throb in anticipation. He brought his mouth back to hers and reversed their positions, covering her body with his as he feasted. He wanted to bury himself deep inside her, to feel her tightness surround him, squeeze him, drive him insane. But he kept reminding himself that it had been a while for her, that he needed to slow things down, make sure she was ready, and that she really wanted what he was offering.

He palmed her, and when he found her slick and dripping, the small amount of control he'd been hanging onto by a slim thread, quickly slipped and he lost it. He had his head between her legs in an instant, lapping at the pool of her arousal, the honeyed sweetness like nothing he'd ever tasted.

His tongue licked and teased, setting a tortuous pace as he traced her clit, pushing the tight bundle of nerves past their limit and sending her flying. But he didn't stop, he wanted more, had to have more from her, and when he took her up again, she bucked against him, fighting for control and quickly losing the battle. And when he pushed two fingers inside her, she exploded, her walls tightening down on him so hard and fast that he couldn't move, his fingers prisoners in her vise-like grip.

He began kissing up her body, leaving a trail of wet from where her orgasm clung to his thickening beard. As her body began to relax, to let go of his fingers at last, he positioned his cock at her entrance and hesitated as he looked deep into her eyes.

"Lexi..."

She didn't give him time to finish his thought. She pushed up against him, pulled his hips toward her, and took him in, watching as his dark, cautious eyes went blind with sinful pleasure. The breath he'd been holding expelled in a rush, a full-body punch to his lungs that left him weak. He filled her, his hard length and thick girth pushing and stretching her to her limits. He held still, enjoying her heat, her tightness, his heart pounding, and when at last he began to move, she met him stroke for stroke.

Their bodies came together, a slow, sensual dance, satisfying needs they'd each long denied with their give and take. Her arms snaked around his neck and pulled his lips to hers. He ravaged her mouth with long, greedy kisses, tongues tasting and teasing while his cock plunged deep.

They took each other higher, gave each other mind-boggling pleasure, and when he felt her orgasm rising from deep within, his own began to build in tandem. They raced to completion, pushing and pulling each other up the steep incline of the mountain and over the top into a sea of drowning ecstasy. Their breath labored and their hearts galloped as he emptied himself inside her, filling her with his cum as her muscles contracted around him, milking him for every last drop.

He kissed her softly, tenderly as he pulled out of her and stretched his sweat-slickened body next to hers. Quiet fell around them as their bodies slowly came down from their high. His thoughts raced as he tried to find the right words, but they wouldn't come. When she shifted and sat up to leave, he blurted the first thing that came to his mind.

"Stay. Will you stay with me, Lexi?"

She hadn't been expecting him to say anything, much less to ask her to stay. Part of her had wanted to, had hoped he'd want her to, and the other part of her told her to run as far and fast as she could without ever looking back. But when she looked in his eyes, she saw turmoil there, was certain the same was reflected in her own eyes, and she understood his need for closeness, to be physically close to anyone, even a stranger.

With a nod of agreement, she laid down again and rolled to her side. When she felt him shift to put his arm around her waist and pull her back to rest against his chest, she went willingly. As he began to drift back to sleep, she felt his warm breath as it feathered across her neck. She closed her eyes and tried not to think of another time, another place, another set of arms.

Lexi slowly woke to the sun streaming in through the window and was confused at first as to why she was in her guest room. When memories of the night before came flooding back, she jerked fully awake and sat up quickly, only to look around and discover that she was alone. She sighed with relief that she would be spared the morning after awkwardness for a little longer.

She slipped out of bed and hurried to her room to dress for the day. Realizing that she was getting a late start she rushed down the stairs, added her boots and coat to shield her from the bitter cold of the morning, and was on her way out the door when she met him coming inside with his arms loaded with milk and eggs.

"What are you doing?"

"Well, you were sleeping hard, so I thought I'd help, maybe let you sleep in a little longer."

"You didn't have to do that, Blaze."

"No," he grinned, "but I did it anyway." He handed her the milk as he pulled his boots off and then started toward the kitchen to store the eggs. She stared at him in disbelief as she followed behind.

"Really, you should have just woken me. I told you, I'm used to doing all this myself."

"Just because you're used to it doesn't mean you can't accept a little help. Besides, I owe you room and board." He turned and winked at her, "I haven't done much to earn my keep."

"Blaze..."

"Stop. It's done and you got a bit of a break. Let it go, Lexi."

She let out an exasperated sigh, "Fine."

They began putting breakfast together, working in companionable silence and as they sat down to eat, they glanced at each other nervously, unsure what needed to be said of the night before. When the silence became unbearable, he began trying to formulate his words.

"Lexi..."

"Don't." She dropped her fork on her plate as she sat back in her chair and watched his face. "Don't you dare apologize for last night. I can see the apology in your eyes, hear it in your voice, and you're going to piss me right the fuck off. I'm not some damsel in distress or some maiden whose virtue you stole. There were two people in that bed last night and both of them were willing and wanting. We took comfort from each other at a time when we both needed it. It's done and over."

Stunned, he looked down at his food and realized he'd been pushing it around on his plate again instead of eating. After a moment, he looked up at her, giving her his crooked grin, the one that lit up his eyes and made her heart flutter. "You were amazing, are amazing. I can't say I've ever met anyone quite like you."

She returned a smile of her own, "Same goes."

With breakfast done, dishes cleared, and the kitchen set to rights, Lexi retreated to her studio and Blaze, finding he was rather enjoying the absence of electronics, stretched out on the couch with the novel he'd started the day before.

He was lost inside King's suspenseful, and terror-filled hotel in The Shining, heart racing as he read the words of murder, mayhem, and insanity when a loud knock came from the front door.

Startled, he dropped the book, cursing before scrambling to return to reality. When the knock happened again, he went to answer the door and was met by a tall, dark-haired man on the other side, hand poised to continue knocking should no answer have come.

"Who the hell are you?"

"Uh, I suppose I could ask you the same? I'm Blaze."

The man pushed his way inside as he continued demanding answers. "Where's Lexi? In her studio?"

"Well, gee," Blaze rolled his eyes as the man walked past him and into the living room, "please come in, make yourself at home."

The man continued as if he hadn't heard him and began yelling for Lexi as he made his way toward her studio at the back of the house. Blaze, hot on his heels, felt his temper begin to flare at the audacity of the stranger who had pushed his way into the house. "Lexi! You alright? Lexi?" He barged into the studio startling her out of the artistic realm she'd been indulging in as she'd painted her feelings on a fresh canvas.

"David? What are you doing here?"

"Lexi. Damn it! Are you alright? Who is this guy?"

"I'm fine, I'm fine." She shook her head and chuckled at the man before her. "David, this is Blaze. Blaze, this is David. David is a friend of mine who lives about a mile from here and drops in from time to time to see if I'm alive or in need of anything. Blaze," she turned to face David, "wrecked his car and is staying with me until a tow truck can make its way up the mountain to dig him out."

She set her paintbrush in a jar of water so that the acrylic wouldn't adhere to the bristles while she dealt with the intrusion. "Now that that is all settled, would the two of you mind lowering the testosterone level in here? It's a little overwhelming." She smiled back and forth between the two men and seeing that neither intended to fully let down their guard, threw her hands up and walked away, leaving them standing and staring each other down with looks of distrust.

With a final sneer, David exited the room and went in search of Lexi. Blaze stood there a moment more, hands on hips chastising himself for acting like an over-protective fool. He hardly knew her, didn't know what kind of relationship she might have with the man who had, in Blaze's mind, invaded their privacy. He kicked himself, knowing that he'd have to try to make amends for his behavior. She'd been nothing but trusting, kind, and giving. He felt like a complete ass.

He found them in the kitchen, David on a stool at the island countertop with a cup of coffee in hand; Lexi pulling out ingredients for some baked good or another, mixing bowls and pans. Blaze walked straight to the coffee pot and helped himself. He grabbed the other stool and sat next to David, watching as Lexi ignored them both.

"I, uh, I'm sorry I acted so badly there, Blaze. From what Lexi just told me it seems you went through quite an ordeal."

Betrayal surged through him and turned his normally laughing eyes hard and cold. When Lexi looked back at him, her own eyes widened in trepidation. But when David continued, Blaze quickly realized that Lexi hadn't betrayed his confidences after all.

"Some of the new hunting regulations have discouraged hunters and the deer have become overpopulated.

I came up the other side of the mountain, so I didn't see your truck. Sounds like you messed it up good."

"Yeah. It's definitely going to need quite a bit of work. Damn it. It's brand new." Disgust rang in his voice and had Lexi smiling at him as she realized the impending crisis had been averted.

"I suppose I could take a look, see if we can get it pulled out? See if maybe we can get it running and you on your way?"

"I appreciate that, but it's alright. The snow has begun to melt some, and the tow service said they'd probably be able to get up here tomorrow." He took a sip of coffee as he contemplated. "How'd you manage to get up here in all this snow?"

"David has a snowmobile. It makes it easy for him to go and check on all the neighbors up and down our little mountain when we have these storms hit. He's very thoughtful and we really appreciate it." She smiled at David as she asked, "How's Melinda doing?"

"She's alright." His pleasant expression turned melancholy. "No real change. Although, she did manage to walk to the mailbox last week without a panic attack. That's an improvement, right?"

"Absolutely. That's wonderful! Maybe it's a step in the right direction?"

"I sure hope so." He turned to Blaze, "My wife suffers from agoraphobia. We, uh, we lost our baby boy about a year ago and she hasn't been the same since. She was six months pregnant when she delivered him. Stillborn. She blames herself; swears she must have done something to have caused it. She's barely been out of the house since the day I brought her home from the hospital. Sometimes just the thought of going on the porch can bring on an attack."

"Wow. I can't imagine how horrible that must be for her, for both of you."

"It isn't easy." He took his empty mug to the sink and turned to Lexi. "Thanks for the coffee. Are you sure you don't need anything? You know I don't mind helping out."

"I appreciate that, David. But I'm good. Please give Melinda my best, alright?"

"Sure. You know how to reach me if something comes up." He started out of the kitchen, nodded his head once at Blaze, and a moment later they heard the sound of his snowmobile starting, the echo of the engine dissipating as it traveled down the snowy lane.

Blaze sipped his coffee as he watched Lexi put the first sheet of cookies in the oven. She set the timer and turned to him. They both began talking at once.

"Lexi..."

"Blaze..."

He chuckled. "Sorry, you go first."

The sigh that left her body said it all to him. "I know you thought I'd told him about your past. I wouldn't do that. I try never to betray confidences. There's enough hurt in this world without adding to it unnecessarily."

"I know that. I figured it out. I apologize for even thinking it, for my initial reaction. And I apologize for getting territorial when he barged in here. I'm not certain what came over me." He frowned into his coffee cup, threw back the last of it, and grimaced as it settled uncomfortably on his stomach. "I had no right."

She didn't say anything, didn't know what to say. With a slight nod of acknowledgment, she turned back to her baking and began filling another sheet with the last of the cookie dough. She'd just placed the final cookie on the sheet when she sensed him behind her. Before she could react, he had a hand on her hip pulling her against him, the hard arousal of his erection pressed to her back.

She'd pulled her hair up and the long line of her neck tempted him. He wrapped his other arm around her, pulling her more securely against him, and with nothing more than his tongue, he licked a slow, sensuous trail of wet heat from the base of her neck up to her ear. When he gently sucked her earlobe, the breath she hadn't been aware she'd been holding exhaled on a heady moan.

"Tell me to stop, Lexi. Tell me to go, to walk away. Tell me you don't want this." His words, whispered seductively in her ear, turned her insides to jelly, made her weak in the knees. She knew they shouldn't, that it would only complicate things, but she couldn't do it, she couldn't form the words. She wanted him, wanted to feel the heat and pleasure he offered one more time. She turned and jumped in his strong arms wrapping her long legs around his torso and met his mouth with her own.

She felt greedy taking so much from him, though he was offering, though she knew he wanted it as much as she did. No matter how much she told herself that it was alright, that they were both using each other, and were simply filling a void, she'd never had sex so casually. She wasn't certain how she felt about it. When he deepened the kiss and all but purred his satisfaction, all thoughts of why she shouldn't disappeared.

He turned and sat her on the island countertop, stripping her out of the thin t-shirt she wore, and groaned when green satin and lace, an exact match to her eye color, teased him as it playfully covered her full, firm breasts. He thought he might lose his mind as he looked his fill. The deep valley between the taut mounds called to him and he went willingly, licking and kissing, burying his face and relishing the softness.

Her supple skin taunted him with the citrusy scent of her shower gel, making him want to lick her from head to toe. His rough hands traced her body, causing her heart rate to spike as they explored. She reached for the hem of his T-shirt and began sliding it up his powerful body. He raised his head long enough for her to peel the tight material from him, and when she tossed his shirt to the side he stood, chest heaving in anticipation under her penetrating gaze as her eyes roamed up and down his body.

When she reached out a hand and began tracing his tattoos, he threw his head back and relished the feel of her fingers as they took a journey across the colorful madness he'd had permanently etched onto his skin. She explored the lines and curves, the angles and swirls, each one telling a story, telling his story, mark by mark. When she rubbed her thumbs across his nipples and teased the barbell piercings there, his cock jumped in response, aching to be inside her.

When he could take it no longer, he grabbed her hands and raised each to his lips, kissing her knuckles and making her quiver with desire. In one swift move, he plucked her from the countertop and carried her to the living room. He sat on the deep sofa and settled her in a straddle across his lap, pulling her into a heated kiss as he did so.

With a quick flick of the wrist, he had her bra unfastened and her breasts bared to him. His mouth found her nipples, drawing each hard peak into his mouth with deep, greedy pulls, and when his teeth teasingly grazed her, her breath caught once again. As he teased and tortured, her body responded with sensual moans that made him growl her name. "Lexi..."

Ravenous. He was simply ravenous for her and all she would give him.

Her hips rocked against him searching for the hardness that strained against his jeans. She reached for the waistband and as her fingers grazed his stomach, his body quivered, and his muscles anxiously flexed with ticklish anticipation. Realizing the effect she had on him made her grin mischievously and she took his mouth with her own, licking inside, teasing and tangling with his tongue.

Before she quite knew what had happened, he had her stripped out of the remainder of her clothing and when she freed him, he raised his hips so she could rid him of the jeans blocking their path to each other. Solid steel waited beneath the velvety softness of his skin and when she lowered herself onto him, they both gasped as they were swamped with pleasure.

Her slick, wet heat surrounded him, and he filled her fully. Thrust for thrust they met, a perfect joining. When he felt her walls begin to tremble and tighten, he sat back and watched, enjoying the way her body flushed as she pleasured herself on his body and rode out her orgasm. Before she had a chance to come down from the high, he laid her back on the sofa, pulled out of her, and buried his face between her legs.

His tongue was wicked as he worked her, licking her, savoring the remnants of her orgasm. He circled her clit, loving the feel of the taut nub as her next orgasm began to build. Over and over, he brought her to the brink and slowly backed off, teasing and tormenting her, taking her to the edge time after time until she could no longer hold back. When she finally came, when at last he finally let her, it was explosive. Her body surged and she saw stars as her head spun with the intensity of the pleasure that slammed into her.

He couldn't think. His mind raced. He needed back inside her, needed to lose himself in her. She was limp in his arms as he positioned her on her knees and entered her from behind. He grabbed her hips and began working her, his body slamming into hers as he fucked her hard and fast. He set a punishing speed, his hips pistoning his cock inside her until he finally felt his own orgasm building.

And when he reached his climax, when his cock stiffened and began to fill her with his cum, he pulled her up to him, kissing her neck as his hands found her breasts again. When she tilted her head back and offered her lips, he took them willingly, greedily. He took everything she offered, leaving them both replete and weakened with sexual satisfaction.

They didn't speak. No words were necessary. They knew that what each had offered had been nothing more than solace, companionship to chase away the loneliness, and a means to fulfill sexual desires.

Later that night they came together again, each searching the other out for reasons they kept to themselves. Then they fell asleep tangled together in her wide bed with a sliver of moonlight peeking through the now partially cleared glass of the skylight.

When Lexi woke late the next morning, the animals had been tended, a pot of coffee waited, and he was gone. All that remained of him was a brief note left on the counter thanking her for her kindness and a phone number.

As Lexi read the note, the still silence of the house echoed around her, and she walked over to her back windows to stare out at her haven. Tears filled her eyes but she didn't let them fall, blinking them back before they could spill down her cheeks. Then with a sigh, she squared her shoulders and crumpled the note in her fist before turning to begin her day.

Chapter Six

Blaze sat in his attorney's office reading over the stack of real estate documents that had been placed in front of him one more time before he began to sign on the dotted line. Page after page of signature lines waited for his lopsided scrawl to be inked on them. Excitement coursed through his body with the knowledge of what he was about to do.

He'd spent the better part of four months searching for exactly what he wanted and just as he'd been about to give up, he'd stumbled across the twenty-acre mountain parcel that was on the verge of belonging to him. It was undeveloped, uncleared, but it had an amazing view or, would have, by the time he was finished with it. And though it wasn't located exactly on the top of a mountain as he'd hoped, there were no neighbors around for several miles.

When he'd gone to inspect the property, he had stepped out of his truck and immediately pictured his house. There would be quite a bit of work to be done before building could begin, but he could see it. A beautiful two-story log cabin, dark wood, and glass, smoke billowing from a chimney in the winter, a small garden in the summer, even an old hound dog curled up by a rocker on a wrap-around porch.

And though he hadn't heard from Lexi since the day he'd left, he couldn't help but think about her every time he imagined what his house would be like. And every time he thought of her, he mentally kicked himself for being an ass - for not calling her, for not checking in to see how she was doing, but most of all, for walking away from her the way he had.

Part of him had been afraid; afraid to call, afraid to hope. Now, he thought, as he began to sign his name, there was nothing he wanted more than to see her and hear her sweet voice one more time.

The day he'd left had been a whirlwind of emotions he hadn't known how to handle in any other way but to run. He'd woken early that morning with a slightly unsettled feeling that something had changed – changed inside him and between the two of them. He hadn't been sure, still wasn't sure what all those changes were, though he thought they had been changes for the better.

As he'd been standing under the steamy hot spray of his shower that morning, he'd been smacked in the face with the reality that he felt rested for the first time in too long to remember. He'd slept. He'd slept without nightmares. He'd slept without waking up – not once. No demons had chased him in the night. No terror had brought him anguish. And yet, that change wasn't the only thing that had happened, not the only thing he'd felt that morning.

There was something else that had changed that he hadn't been able to pinpoint at the time. And though he hadn't known what it was, it had reeked of danger. And instead of sticking around to try to figure it out, he'd left.

For the first time in his life, he'd turned away from the danger instead of running toward it. He'd hurried through the morning chores wanting to get them done so that Lexi wouldn't have to tend to them. And when he'd finished and realized she still slept, he'd gathered his things, written her a note and walked down to wait for the tow truck.

As he'd ridden down the mountain staring out the passenger side window of the tow truck, his disabled vehicle hitched to the back like a sad child being forced to leave a toy store, his instincts had told him that though leaving the way he had seemed cowardly, it was for the best. Those instincts, those same instincts that had kept him safe on numerous missions, had pricked at his conscience all morning, a warning sign that something bad was going to happen if he didn't leave. Since then, the feeling had slowly faded, leaving behind doubts about the reliability of his intuition and making him laugh at his paranoia.

Looking back at the way he'd left had made him feel like shit, like a coward, but at the time all that had been on his mind was the feeling that he'd needed to run, to leave, and do so as quickly as possible as Lexi's safety had somehow depended on it. And now? Well, now that apprehension had faded, and he wanted nothing more than to drive back up the mountain and see her again.

He wanted to share everything with her about the property, the house he'd finally worked out a design for, all his plans. He wanted to thank her in person one more time for her caring, her generosity, and to tell her that soon he would be close by if she ever needed anything. Very close. In fact, thinking about just how close they would be to each other brought a happy and wicked grin to his face.

When his real estate agent had called to tell him about the property that had been listed for sale, he'd been excited. Finding out that the tract of land had been on Lexi's mountain had thrilled him. It was located further down the mountain than her little piece of heaven, and with the switchbacks would still be at least a half-hour drive between their properties, but he would be close. Close enough that they could, he hoped, cultivate a friendship. And if luck stayed on his side, if she could ever forgive him for leaving the way he had, maybe they could even be more than friends.

He felt they had connected, not just sexually, though that had been amazing, but on a level that others might never understand. Trauma, he thought, had a way of tying people together, even when there were no other commonalities.

After he'd left Lexi, he'd taken steps to learn the best ways to handle his PTSD. Leaping out of his comfort zone and talking to a therapist had been one of the most difficult, and at times excruciating, things he'd done in his life. He'd gone to therapy weekly, and after a rocky start of not knowing what to say, had eventually opened up, sharing what he could and his feelings about all he'd gone through.

He still made a weekly visit to the therapist, and while he acknowledged he had a long way to go in his recovery, he now knew some of his worst triggers and what to do, how best to handle them, when they couldn't be avoided. The nightmares no longer chased him, and he'd had his eyes opened to the good that he'd done during his time in service. The good he'd done, he now realized, had far outweighed the bad that had haunted him for so long. He'd finally been able to put the devastating loss of his friend to rest, counting their friendship as one of the positives in his life.

Now, as Blaze repeatedly signed his name, a swirl of ink scrawled upon line after line of a thick packet of legalese, his heart soared. When he signed the last page, the last bit of darkness that had lingered around the edges of his psyche faded into the background and was replaced by the shimmering brightness of his future.

Lexi stopped hammering nails long enough to stretch out her back and ease her muscles. She'd been at it for hours and while the repairs she was making weren't overly strenuous, the angle that she'd had to assume to maneuver the last few boards in place had been odd and uncomfortable.

Winter had been hard, and the snowfalls had averaged higher than normal totals. It had taken its toll on the shed, and while replacing the roof had been on her Spring to-do list, she'd had to move up the timeline after the most recent storm had blown through. The wind and rain had been strong enough that it had ripped half the weakened shed roof off and deposited the debris around her yard. Clean-up had been a bitch, but after several hours of picking up limbs, shingles and other roofing materials, she'd finally returned her yard to some semblance of order.

David had helped; she took a moment to think of how much of a blessing her neighbor had been. He'd made the rounds after the storm, checking in with all the neighbors, as usual, helping where needed. He'd done a fence repair for one neighbor, and tree removal for another. She could have gotten the work done without him, but the clean-up had definitely gone faster with the help of her compassionate friend. She was thankful to have him around.

With the last board in place, Lexi climbed down the ladder and surveyed her work. She'd made the decision to change from roofing shingles to a metal roof and the delivery truck was due that afternoon. David had promised to come help with that portion of the repair, and she was grateful, once again, for his kindness. She wasn't sure if it was just the kind of people David and his wife were or if it was ingrained in the people of West Virginia, but it helped to solidify her belief that she'd ended up exactly where she was meant to be when her world had fallen apart.

She started toward the house to grab a drink when she heard the sound of a smooth engine climbing her long driveway. It didn't sound like the diesel engine of David's truck, and it wasn't quite time for her delivery yet, so she wondered who it could be. Curious, she stood watching for the vehicle to come into view. When the red truck rounded the last bend, a tingling started at the base of her neck and her heartbeat quickened. Well, she thought, what have we here?

Flashes of the last few hours they'd spent together strobed through her mind in quick succession. When she'd woken to find him gone, part of her had been relieved and part of her had been desperately disappointed. Though they'd essentially been strangers, and his stay had been short, she'd gotten used to having him there. When she'd closed herself off from the world, she'd closed herself off to things that most people take for granted. She hadn't realized just how much she had missed the every day of being around other people on a regular basis until Blaze had appeared.

After they'd gotten past the initial awkwardness of the situation, she'd enjoyed having someone to share a meal with, to sit and chat with over a glass of wine. She'd even enjoyed the companionable silence they'd shared as they'd sat in front of the fire and read. And, she thought, she'd thoroughly enjoyed his body and the long-ago-forgotten desires he'd re-awakened in her. In the silence he'd left behind, she'd come to the realization that she no longer wanted to live a life of solitude.

The walls she'd built around her heart after Jackson and her parents had died, had cracked and were slowly starting to crumble, leaving her feeling more vulnerable than she had in years. She hadn't thought she'd been lonely until Blaze had popped into her world, twisting her thoughts and emotions into a whirlwind of feelings she'd thought could and would never be resurrected, then swirling back out as quickly as he'd come. But when she'd woken and realized he was gone, that loneliness had become abundantly clear, a deafening siren of silence.

She'd tried not to be pissed that he'd left the way he did. After all, they owed each other nothing, not even an explanation as there'd been no expectations, no promises. Yet knowing he could just leave without saying goodbye in person had irked her more than she'd cared to admit.

She could have called him, had wanted to, had wanted desperately to hear his voice, but each time she'd picked up the phone she'd changed her mind. Doubts had snuck into her thoughts and had her questioning if he'd just left his number out of guilt rather than genuine interest. No longer than she'd spent with him, she'd determined he was a man of his word, a man with a conscience, and though he had no reason to feel guilty for the things they'd done, it would be just like him to let those self-destructive thoughts eat at him. The call she'd wanted to make had gone unmade day after day, night after night.

In the time he'd been gone, she'd begun to venture out more, making more trips to town, to the hardware store, to the grocery herself, rather than the mail orders and deliveries she'd become accustomed to. The steps had been small and had taken their toll on her at first, but she'd powered through until it was easier and easier. Their time together had opened a part of herself that she'd previously closed off, and that opening had been just wide enough that she'd finally begun to live again rather than simply existing.

Now she watched as he drove the last few feet up the drive and giggled to herself as she tried to imagine how exactly he would try to cover his ass and the awkward way he'd walked away. As he parked the truck and slowly climbed out of the seat, he seemed unsure of himself, and the thought that he might be nervous gave her a small amount of satisfaction. He watched her with wariness, a hint of longing, and she wondered once again, just exactly what had brought him back up the mountain, back into her life.

More importantly, she wondered what exactly she planned to do about it.

"Lexi." He stood hipshot, hands in pockets, trying to appear casual as he looked her over from head to toe. His heart, already beating rapidly at just the thought of being in her presence again, skipped a beat when he looked into her vibrant green eyes. He wasn't certain how it could be possible, but she seemed even more radiant than the day he'd left her, her head on her pillow while the barest hint of dawn had peeked through the windows.

"Blaze." Damn, he looks good, she thought. Could it be that he was even sexier than she remembered?

"I, uh, I hope you don't mind me showing up without notice, but I wanted, hoped, that I could talk to you." He ran his hand over the back of his neck as he stumbled over his words. Nerves he hadn't realized were on edge began to fuck with his mind.

Though the thought of making him suffer greatly appealed to her, she found she didn't have it in her to be petty. "I need something to drink. You've come this far, so you might as well come on in and join me."

"Alright."

He walked behind her, watching as she climbed the steps, enjoying the view of her walking away just as much as he had of her coming towards him. He'd noted tiredness just around the edges of her eyes and wondered what she had been doing with herself over the past couple of months. He looked around her yard, saw where she had obviously been working on her shed, along with a few changes here and there from what he remembered of the brief time he'd spent as a guest in her home.

Spring looked good on Lexi's mountain, he thought. The oak, pine, and maple trees lining her property had begun to fill in and green up nicely. Her flower beds were a riot of colors, textures, and scents. He saw hyacinths, daffodils, and tulips, and so many more plants and blooms he didn't recognize, had no names for. He took a deep breath and tried to identify some of the scents floating on the breeze, but they all blended, one smell rolling into the next, a sweet and refreshing perfume.

Birds swooped and soared, singing as they searched for food and material to build their nests. Squirrels chased each other up trees, chattering as they went, disappearing in knot holes. Mating season, it seemed, was in full swing. It reminded him of Bambi and the line about everybody being twitterpated when spring arrives. That, he decided, was an apt description of what he felt when he looked at Lexi. Twitterpated.

He followed her to the kitchen and sat on one of the high-backed stools at the island. Flashes of ravishing her as she sat on the countertop made his body tingle and flush with longing. He watched as she poured lemonade into tall clear glasses and offered him one. He took a drink and stared as she did the same with her own, following the line of her neck and throat as she drank half the liquid without taking a breath. When she sat the glass down, crossed her arms, and leaned against the countertop, she stared into his eyes, making him itch even more to get his hands on her.

"So, what did you want to talk about, Blaze? You could have called, you know. It would have saved you a long trip up here."

He brushed aside her aloofness and his crooked smile lit his face as he spoke. "I found it, Lexi. I found my haven."

"What? Oh, that's wonderful!" Despite the irritation she felt at the way he'd left, genuine happiness for him brought a smile of her own, and she reached out to take his hands in hers, squeezing them in congratulations and understanding.

She remembered the excitement and contentment she'd felt when she'd found her own property. That feeling of finally finding where she needed to be had overwhelmed her, but it had been quickly followed by blissful peace. It had been the sanctuary she'd so desperately needed.

"It's exactly what I was looking for. I searched and searched, getting nowhere, and as I was about to give up, it just suddenly appeared. My agent called me the moment it was listed. It is the perfect spot. There are no neighbors around for a couple of miles, so once I have my place built, I'll be able to have that solitude we talked about. Time. I'll have time to think, to process, to just be. I'll have time to build something to call my own, something to be proud of."

"It sounds perfect!"

"There's more, Lexi."

"Oh, really? What's that?"

"Yeah. The property isn't far from here. It's actually only about a half-hour away." A shiver tap danced down her spine as she processed what he'd said. "Will you take a ride with me? I really want to show it to you. I feel like I wouldn't be where I am had it not been for you, and I...I just need to share it with you."

"Wow. I'd love to see it." Just then she remembered the delivery. "Oh, but I have a delivery truck coming soon. I can't leave until they unload my metal. Do you mind waiting?"

"No. Not at all. I have nowhere else to be, nowhere else I want to be. I saw all the work you've done out there. Everything looks great, Lexi. I don't know what I expected as the only time I'd seen your place it was snow-covered, but I can tell you that it wasn't what I see out there now. It's gorgeous, picture perfect."

"Thanks." She told him about the storm, the damage, and all the clean-up. "Luckily, David came up and helped. If he hadn't, I'd probably still be trying to pick up limbs and getting organized."

At the mention of David's name, his instincts kicked in and alarms began to sound. He chastised himself for thinking bad things about the man. He couldn't figure out why a perfectly nice man, a helpful man, a married man, caused him to be so protective of Lexi, but those warning bells were ringing loud and clear. There was something about David that made him uneasy, to say the least. He tried to push the thoughts out of his head but when Lexi continued, it was all he could do not to crush the fragile glass he held.

"Actually, David may be here soon. He told me he intended to come help with the shed roof."

"Lexi. How well do you know David?"

"What? Why?"

"Humor me."

"Gosh. I've known him and his wife for several years now. They moved to the mountain about a year or so after me. They're very nice people."

"What can you tell me about his wife?"

"Well, she never comes up with him anymore – the agoraphobia is too extreme. She just can't manage to leave their house. But she almost always sends David with some kind of food she's prepared. I think cooking and baking are her outlets, the way she has chosen to process and work through their loss."

"The agoraphobia – he said it started when their baby died, right?"

"Yes. It was so hard on them. Melinda, well, I can only imagine how difficult life has been for her since then. I went down to visit with her a few days after they were home from the hospital, but she couldn't even bring herself to answer the door."

"I'm sorry to hear that."

"I know. Actually, I haven't even seen her since before she miscarried."

"Wait. What? That was what? Over a year ago, right?"

"Yeah. I've gone down to visit, to check on her, but she has such a hard time with it. She won't answer the door or, on the occasions that David has been there and answered, she's been resting, and I haven't wanted to disturb her."

The warning bells began ringing harder, louder, causing the back of his neck to begin tingling. He rubbed absently at it as he tried to figure out why those bells were resonating so loudly. Something, he thought, was off about the whole situation.

He was about to question her further when they heard the arrival of the delivery truck. They both stood on the deck and watched as the materials were unloaded. She signed for the delivery and then watched as the emptied truck drove off. She couldn't help but be a little excited that one more thing on her to-do list was about to be checked off, and a little excited at how nice the property would look, once again.

Blaze watched as her face lit up in anticipation. He understood completely. There was something so satisfying about knowing what you wanted and seeing those wants take shape, come to life. And at that moment, with the sun shining down on her red hair, glinting off the loose curls, with the smile that not only brightened her features, but gleamed in her eyes, the last piece to his puzzle fell in place. He knew what he wanted. He wanted, needed, his hands on her again. He wanted, needed, more from her than he'd even realized before he'd driven back up the mountain.

"Lexi..."

She turned to him and saw the flames of desire burning in his eyes. Though she wanted him too, she felt they needed to take a few steps back. There were things that needed saying, explanations to be given, and she wasn't sure where all that might lead. Time, she thought, they needed time to get to know each other before they jumped back into bed, no matter how much she wanted him. They needed time to see if they were compatible under normal circumstances, not just under forced situations. He reached for her, and she took a cautious step back.

"Don't. Please." She turned her back to him and looked out over her yard. Her thoughts and emotions swirled, an internal storm that had her stomach in knots. She felt she'd been on a bit of a rollercoaster with him since that winter day that he'd crashed into her life. And she'd thought recently, with his disappearing act and the space it had provided, that the ride had possibly been coming to an end.

But with his sudden appearance, the fact that he'd chosen to come in person to share his news, and the wanton desire she'd just seen radiating off him in waves of lust, she now realized that the ride was far from over. It had instead just been a lull, a straight section of track that had given her a false sense of completeness. Now that rollercoaster had started climbing a steep incline and she needed to make a decision. Should she hit the emergency brake and get off the ride, or should she prepare to plunge off the other side? Her stomach flipped in uncertain anticipation.

"I'm sorry, Lexi. I...Well, maybe I shouldn't have come."

"No. It isn't that." She looked back at him. "I want that. I want you. I really want to be with you. I'm not jumping at the opportunity to be with you again partly because I want to be with you so badly. I'm afraid, Blaze. We shared a few very intense days, and I enjoyed our time together - once we got past the awkwardness, that is." She smiled at him. "But I'm afraid I want this and the potential of this, too much.

"You have to remember that before you, there had only been one person that I'd been with intimately, sexually. I thought I would be spending my life with that man, but instead, I lost him, and then I lost myself. I'm still trying to find myself and I'm afraid that if I jump in too quickly with you, I'll never be found. I'm afraid I'll simply sink and never resurface. I'm afraid I'll never be myself again. Do you understand?"

He sighed, "Yes. Yes, I do." He'd worked through scenario after scenario on his drive up the mountain. He'd wondered what her reaction would be to seeing him again, what her reaction would be to hearing why he'd had to leave and leave just the way he had. He'd wondered if she would even listen to him and give him a chance to explain. "How about this? How about you come and take that drive with me so I can show you my land? When I bring you back, I'll help you get that roof done. We can talk. I have things I want to tell you - things I need to tell you." He bowed his head and closed his eyes as he muttered, "I have things I need to explain."

She sighed as she considered, "Alright. I'd love to see your property."

He took her by the hand and escorted her to the truck, opening the door for her and closing her inside. He hurried around the front and was about to open his door when he caught a movement off to the north side of her yard. He stood for a minute trying to figure out what he'd seen, what had caused his defensive instincts to momentarily kick in, but there was nothing. And though he didn't see anything, the sudden stillness that had taken over the atmosphere left him with a sick feeling in the pit of his stomach. He gave another look around and still seeing nothing unusual, climbed in the truck and started down the steep curves of the driveway.

Quietness hung in the air of the cab of the truck as they began their trek, curve meeting curve as they twisted and wound their way down the forested mountainside. They hadn't gone too far when they passed a little house tucked into a small glade, the surrounding yard immaculate and tidy. And though the house was weather-worn and desperate for a coat of paint, purple and pink pansies in full bloom filled window boxes and gave the house a homey look.

"That's David and Melinda's place."

Blaze gave the dingy house another once over, taking note that something eerie lurked beneath the stillness of the surface. He wasn't sure exactly what that something was, but something was off about the property. Something, he felt, was off about David, Melinda, and their whole situation. But he kept those somewhat baseless thoughts to himself as they continued on their journey.

Lexi pointed out several other landmarks along the way and Blaze stored every bit of information she passed along in his steel trap of a mind. When they reached his property at last, butterflies swarmed in his stomach. He couldn't say why, but Lexi's opinion of his land, of his plans, meant a great deal to him.

He stopped the truck at a wide spot in the road and looking out the passenger window, pointed out the boundary lines, gave her a description of what his plans were. He talked of the area to be cleared, the as-yet unformed driveway, the house he planned to build, and various other ideas he'd had. When he spoke of the house, he reached in the backseat of the truck and pulled out a set of plans for her to look at, walking her through every aspect of his vision.

"Blaze. This is wonderful. It's exactly what you talked about wanting. I'm genuinely happy for you. You deserve this, something of your own, the solitude, but more, you deserve peace and to be happy. I sincerely hope that you find that happiness here."

"I hope I can find that and more." He paused as he considered the best approach. "Lexi, will you come take a walk with me for a minute? This is the first time I've been here since I bought it. I'd really like to wander for a bit."

She nodded her head in agreement and soon they were traipsing through thick brush. They wandered over and around saplings reaching out to touch streaky rays of sun under a thick green canopy. That canopy provided by their fellow trees, trees that had reached their height years and years before, long before the saplings had sprouted and taken root in the rich soil of West Virginia, protected and nurtured those tender shoots in their struggle for survival. They walked with care and when they stepped into a small clearing, he stopped and turned to face her.

"I need to explain something to you, Lexi. I need to explain why I left the way I did."

"Blaze, you don't have to explain anything to me."

"No. Really, I do." He sighed, "I'm an asshole, Lexi. I will never try to say otherwise. But even as much of an asshole as I am, I could never, would never, leave like that without a damn good reason. Not with all that happened between us, not with all we shared."

"Alright." She crossed her arms, an unconscious defense against his words.

"That morning when I woke up, I looked over at you and damn, you were so beautiful lying there. There was just enough moonlight left coming through that skylight and shining softly down on your face, your hair, that I could make out each and every fascinating detail.

"It was all I could do not to reach out and trace your features, the peaceful set of your lips as you slept. In that moment I wanted to kiss you, I wanted to hold you, I wanted to pleasure us both. And as I was laying there looking at you, I started to realize that I felt different. Something was changing inside me, had probably started changing before that moment, even.

"I needed to think so I decided I'd take a shower, get some coffee, do that thinking, and some evaluating. While I was in the shower, I realized something. I had slept that night. I had slept better that night than I had in more years than I could remember. No nightmares. No flashes from the past haunting me. No pain and despair over things that couldn't have been changed no matter how hard I wished they could.

"When all of this dawned on me, my first instinct was that I'd possibly found where I belonged. That I was home, at peace, at long last." He laughed nervously. "I have to admit that it scared the shit out of me. It scared me so much so that I panicked, and all I could think was that I needed to run, to escape. By the time I got out of the shower, gathered my stuff, and went downstairs, the panic had subsided, and I started to feel...happy. I'd started envisioning the possibilities fate had thrown at me and I was as close to being content, at peace, as I'd been in a very long time."

Lexi stood, staring up into his deep, dark eyes, heart pounding as she listened to his explanation.

"I'd had this revolving door of emotions whirling through me in a very short period of time and it freaked me out. Seriously freaked me out. But I made the decision that I needed to talk to you, to see how you felt, to see if there was anything there on your end. So, there I was, enjoying some coffee while I did some more processing, and before I'd even finished my first cup something changed.

"This awareness came over me and I felt like I was being watched. No, that's not quite right, either. I felt like I was being hunted. There were warning bells and flashing red lights. You can't imagine what it was like for me. I'd been scared, happy, freaked out, hopeful, one emotion rolling into the other that morning, when out of nowhere this sense of imminent danger dropped on me. It was like a damn bomb going off in my head, in my heart.

"Lexi. The only times in my life I've felt that was when something really bad was about to happen. It was like this flashing warning sign that I needed to go, and I needed to move quickly. I felt I was in danger, but more, I felt you were in danger because of me. I will gamble with my own life, but I'll never gamble with yours. And that morning, your life depended on me leaving and never looking back.

"Now, I know you think that sounds crazy, but I trust my instincts. Yes, they've been off lately, not working as perfectly as they used to, at least not since I lost my friend. But I couldn't take that kind of chance with you. I couldn't put your life on the line, not for even the slimmest possibility that something might happen to you.

"So, I ran. As I got further and further away from you the fear began to ease, the danger began to fade. When I was finally off the mountain, it disappeared completely. I didn't want to go that morning, didn't want to leave you, but I felt I had to, that I had no choice." He ran a hand over his bald head and stared up at the canopy of leaves as he tried to gather his thoughts. "Is this making any sense?"

"I don't know what to say to you, Blaze." He looked back into her eyes and saw the confusion, the concern. "That's quite a bit to take in."

He laughed, "Yeah. I know. I'm sorry I dumped it on you like that. I just really need you to know, well, everything. There's more. Are you ready or are you still processing?" He grinned as he saw the laughter in her eyes.

"Well, I guess you better tell me the whole of it."

"Right. So, I felt better when I left, but only in the knowledge that me leaving was protecting you. The rest of me? The rest of me felt like I'd lost something, someone who could, who would change my life. It broke another piece of me to leave you. It has haunted me every moment since. I don't know how many times I picked up my phone to call you, to text you. But each time I did I stopped myself. I had so much to say to you, but I really had no idea what or how I wanted to say it to you.

"Instead, I threw all my thoughts and efforts into finding this, into getting my own, into making my own. I began working on me and my needs, putting myself first for once in my life. Lexi, please believe me when I tell you that not one day has passed since I left that I haven't thought about you, wondering. Wondering how you were, what you were doing? Wondering what would happen if I came back? I reached a point where I couldn't stay away any longer. I had to see if I'd imagined everything between us, to see how you felt, Lexi. I want to get to know you better. I want to see if there really is or could be something more between us, because I feel like we could be amazing together."

"Blaze..."

"Wait. There's still more."

She laughed softly, "For someone who would hardly speak when we first met, you sure have gotten chatty."

His crooked grin spread, once again, "I know. It seems you bring it out in me."

"Well, then, let's hear it. All of it."

"Okay." The grin disappeared and his face began to show signs of concern. "Today when we left your house, I got that feeling again. Those warning bells and flashing lights went off. I swear to you I don't know what's causing it, but it worries me. Lexi, I don't want you in danger, but I don't know if I can stay away from you any longer. The thought of being away from you, of not seeing where this might lead, is unbearable."

"Look. I can't imagine that I would be in any danger or trouble. I'm just living my life out on my mountain, minding my own business." She paused as she looked around at the sun-dappled ground, her mind racing. "I mean, I guess anything could happen, but I can't possibly see what would be causing you to feel this way."

"I know. I can't figure it out either." He shoved his hands in the pockets of his jeans and took a long look around at his future. "Lexi. I know you need time to think, but I need to know if you're willing, if there is a chance for us to get to know each other. I think there's something here, something that could be amazing between us." He paused as he looked back at her, hope in his eyes. "I don't know what's causing this feeling of danger, but I promise you, if you give me, give us, a chance, no matter what, I will look out for you. Are you interested in finding out if there could be more between us?"

Chapter Seven

Lexi couldn't take her eyes off him. Everything he'd told her had made her realize just how complex the man standing before her actually was, how much deeper he was than she had given him credit. She could see potential in him, potential in them together, and the thought made her happy, but oh, so wary at the same time. Part of her knew that if she said yes, she would be taking a huge leap of faith, a leap that she wasn't sure she had the ability to successfully make. Part of her, and it seemed to be the part that was making decisions for her, screamed that he was worth it, that the possibility of what they could become and make together would be worth it.

"Blaze, I..." She turned and stared at the peaceful view surrounding them. "I don't know if I can be what you want me to be. I don't know if I have that in me anymore, or that I will ever have it again. When Jackson died, a piece of me died, too. I've been content to live out my life here on the mountain, resigned to my fate.

"When you left that morning, when you left the way you did, I tried not to let it get to me. We hadn't made any promises to each other, and we both knew going in that we were simply looking to fill the loneliness, the hollowness we felt inside. We knew, even without words, that what we were sharing was a small moment in time that eased some of the ache we'd both endured. She looked back at him, then turned and stepped close enough to him that she could feel the heat and energy radiating from his body.

"It was what we needed at the time, but time has marched on like it does, and my needs have changed, your needs have changed, and the things we need from each other have changed. Blaze," she looked hopefully up into his searching eyes, "I don't know that I will ever be whole again, that I will ever be able to give all of myself again. In fact, I don't know how much I have left inside of me to give to anyone, but if you're willing to take that chance, to take whatever I do have to offer, I am, too."

Breath he hadn't been aware he'd been holding rushed from his body and he reached for her, tugging her close and wrapping her in his muscular arms. The kiss they shared was searing, soul-searching, and left them both breathless and hungry for more.

The sun was still high in the sky when they climbed the driveway to Lexi's cabin. True to his word, Blaze jumped into helping finish the shed roof. They hadn't been working long when he looked up to see David climbing out of his truck with an unhappy look on his face. Blaze watched warily from his perch on the roof as Lexi walked over to say hello. He couldn't figure out the reason the man made his skin crawl, but he was determined to find out. He couldn't escape the feeling that David was hiding something.

At that moment he made the decision to do some research and call in a few favors. If there was one positive thing that had come from his time in service, it was that he'd made contacts all over the world and close friends in high places who would be more than willing to do some digging, even off the record.

"Blaze."

"David."

"I see you made it back up the mountain. The truck looks to be in better condition than when I last saw it."

"Yeah. It took a couple of weeks to get the repairs made, but it cleaned up real nice."

"I can finish this up if you need to be on your way."

"Actually, I'm not in any hurry." Blaze looked over at Lexi and grinned. "But if you want to help out that would be great. Between the two of us, we'll have this done in no time."

Lexi rolled her eyes as those testosterone levels climbed again, the two men posturing for her attention. "Ummm, excuse me. There are three of us here."

"True, but if you let us take care of this then you can go and get yourself ready for a night out." The look he shot her had her blood pumping hard in anticipation. "I still need to pay you back for my room and board during the storm."

"Well, no, you don't. But I'm no fool and I haven't had a night out in a long time. So, I think I'll take you up on that offer." Lexi thanked David and made her way in the house, excited for the evening ahead.

The two men worked with barely a word spoken between them. Within a couple of hours, the roof was finished and clean-up complete. Blaze watched David as he drove away, his taillights disappearing down the drive. When he was finally out of sight, Blaze pulled out his phone and made the first in a long series of calls.

Lexi had taken Blaze's suggestion to heart. The time she'd spent soaking in the tub, steamy water and a cool glass of white wine in hand, had relaxed her and she'd taken her time getting ready. She'd expertly styled her red curls in a loose bun, a sexy mess that left the long line of her neck exposed, and the large hoop earrings she chose added the perfect amount of sparkle to draw the eye to that long, sensuous line. What was that old saying, she asked herself? The bigger the hoop, the bigger the 'ho? The mere thought that she'd call herself a 'ho made her giggle.

She'd never had a heavy hand with make-up, and the slight smudging up of her eyes, the couple of swipes of mascara were enough to play up her features without overwhelming her face. A finishing touch of tinted gloss added soft color to her full lips, making them look deliciously kissable.

Her light sweater and blue jeans were form-fitting and hugged her curves in all the right places. Dressed and ready to go, she examined her image in her full-length mirror. She came across as what she'd always been – a country girl with a touch of class, quiet sensuality in a delectable package. And when she walked down the stairs and found Blaze waiting for her, the smile she offered him was heart-stopping.

She knew she'd hit the mark when he couldn't take his eyes off her, his gaze roaming from head to toe and back again and burning with lust and longing.

The mom-and-pop diner they chose sat on the corner of the busiest street in a small town nestled at the base of the mountain and boasted a Saturday night special of Ma's Beef & Dumplins. The dinner announcement written on a small whiteboard located in the vestibule, along with a sign that said "Seat Yo'self!" was welcoming and offered a warm and homey touch to the atmosphere.

A glass display case stood next to the cash register and every shelf was filled with homemade cakes and pies, delectable deserts just waiting to be devoured. A giant picture window was covered with postcards from around the world – a small touch of appreciation from customers through the years as they'd traveled here and there, a chaotic and one-of-a-kind work of art.

A black and white checkerboard pattern ran the length of the diner floor from wall to wall. An old jukebox sat in a corner and played hits from the 50s and 60s softly, while framed and autographed photos of mega stars from those eras hung on the walls. Marilyn Monroe, James Dean, Elvis Presley, Brigitte Bardot, John Wayne, and so many more famous faces graced the walls. And neon signs glowed with pink and blue against posters of classic cars in their prime, a blast from the past.

There were booths and tables to choose from, but tall swivel stools upholstered in red leather stationed beneath a high countertop called to them, and soon they were seated, hip to hip, lost in conversation while the dulcet tones of Frankie Valli and The Four Seasons played softly as they waited for their food to arrive.

They kept their banter light, discussing books, discussing his plans for his house, and even discussing a few moments in time from their childhoods. Juicy cheeseburgers grilled to perfection and crispy fries were washed down with fountain sodas as they flirted and teased. They lingered over dessert - pecan pie and coffee, and between bites Blaze admitted his absolute obsession with the nutty sweetness of the pie. When he ended up finishing not only his slice, but part of hers, Lexi laughed harder than she had in years.

"Tell me about your family, Blaze. You said you grew up in West Virginia. Are they close by?"

"Not much to tell there. My parents moved to Florida about ten years ago to escape the West Virginia winters. Mom spends her days sitting out on the beach or their back deck reading romance novels and drinking iced coffee, and dad spends all his time in his garage. He has all these woodworking tools and keeps promising mom that he'll build this or that for her." Blaze chuckled. "I don't think he has ever completely finished a project he's started. Mom just laughs at him and humors him each time he says he's going to start something new."

Lexi smiled, "Sounds like they have a great relationship."

"They do."

"And what about any siblings?"

"I have a younger brother but we were never very close. I think there was too much of an age difference. By the time he reached an age where I felt we really could have connected, I'd graduated and joined the Navy. We just never really bonded. He lives out in Colorado now and spends his days and nights doing freelance photography."

"Do you ever go see them?"

"My parents, yes. I went shortly after I left here in the winter and spent a couple of weeks with them. It was really good to see them. My brother? Nah. Maybe one of these days I'll go out and see him, try to get to know him and to connect with him, but right now I much prefer to spend my time getting to know you."

When they were done with their meal, they strolled hand-in-hand through the quiet streets, the occasional car slowly ambling by as they enjoyed the cool night breeze and simple and quiet ambiance of small-town USA.

Blaze let his eyes roam, taking in the stillness of the night as they walked along. "I've missed this."

She looked around as she tried to figure out what he was referring to. "What?"

"Normal. I've missed the normality that comes with the day-to-day, the little things that make life worth living, the things that I joined up to fight for in the first place. You know, little things that should always be part of life, like dinner out on a Saturday night with a beautiful, intelligent, sexy woman. Things that mean so much, like shared laughs, a stroll under the stars with someone you care about. Gazing into captivating green eyes and being mesmerized by their depths. Soft, lingering kisses in the moonlight." He stopped and pulled her into a tight embrace. "Lexi. I'm going to kiss you. Right here. Right now."

She smiled as he dipped his head and claimed her lips with his own. His tongue probed gently, licking, teasing her to open for him. She did so willingly, and he deepened the kiss, taking them both under quickly, stirring their desire for each other until they ached for more. Hands roamed as their bodies pressed closely together, drawing out the kiss and heightening those desires, and when she felt the hard length of him begin to grind against her lower belly, her core reached its melting point.

He pulled back and stared into her eyes as their bodies panted and begged for more. Then he leaned in, intending on going back for round two when a shot rang out, shattering the quiet stillness of the night. Pain etched his face as he quickly gathered Lexi to him, cradled her body with his own, and dove for the sidewalk.

"Stay down!"

She might have screamed had the breath not been knocked out of her when they'd landed on the hard concrete, his massive body rolling them so that he covered and protected her, while he cushioned her body as much as possible. Panic had her eyes going wide and her heart racing. She pushed against him, her lungs desperate for air, but he wouldn't budge.

"Damn it, Lexi! I said stay down!"

"Can't breathe," she gasped.

"Shit. Sorry." He eased off her enough that she could take her first full breath since they'd dove for cover but stayed close, doing his best to shield her from whatever madness lurked in the dark. Time crept by as they waited and listened. No more shots were fired, though, and it wasn't long before a small group gathered around them in concern and confusion.

"Holy crap! Someone call 911!"

Blaze jumped up and helped Lexi to her feet. Then he began to look her over, questioning if she was alright.

"Fuck! Are you alright?"

"I'm fine! I promise, Blaze."

"Ok. Good. Yeah, good." Lexi stared up at him noting the wildness that had taken over his eyes, the same wildness that had been there that first night when he'd wrecked and awakened on her couch with no idea where he was or what was going on.

Out of the corner of her eye she saw red begin to drip down his arm and she gasped as she realized he'd been hurt. "Blaze!" She reached out to him hoping she was seeing things. "You're bleeding!" She eased up his sleeve to take a look at his wound and stared in horror before looking around frantically for help. "Oh, God! You've been shot!"

He looked at his arm in confusion, at the streaks of red as they left a trail running down his arm, dripping on the pale gray of the sidewalk. "Fuck. I hate it when that happens." Suddenly, the burning that he hadn't paid attention to before, intensified. He quickly removed his shirt and used it to staunch the blood flow. He glanced down at Lexi and saw shock as it rippled across her face. "Lexi. I'm okay. It just grazed me. I promise I'm fine."

She took his shirt and tied it tightly around the wound, a temporary bandage until help arrived. Her tears began to flow uncontrollably and, helpless, he grabbed her and hugged her close. She wrapped her arms around him and held on, her body shaking uncontrollably as flashes of what could have happened played on repeat through her mind.

It wasn't too long before police and medics arrived. Statements were given and police canvassed the area. Blaze's wound was tended, leaving Lexi nothing to do but pace as he received medical care. Worried about him and completely astonished that they'd been shot at, she slowly walked back and forth, arms wrapped around her stomach in an effort to keep herself together and not lose her mind as she waited to hold him close once more.

"You're lucky this is just a graze. Burned a line right through all that pretty muscle there, handsome." Blaze smiled at the grandmotherly medic as she wrapped his arm and gave him instructions for care. "I'm going to tell you to take it easy but looking at your scars it appears you've dealt with things like this before. How long were you in?"

"Fifteen years."

"That's a long time. Thank you for your service." She taped off the bandage and patted him on the shoulder. "If that gives you any trouble there's a clinic over on Third Street. They'll take a look at it for ya. But I don't think you've got anything to worry about." She looked over to where Lexi paced, concern etched on her face. "Well, nothing but that pretty lady of yours. She looks like she might jump right out of her skin."

"She'll be fine." The steel edge to his voice left no doubts to his determination. "I'm going to make sure of it. I'm going to take care of her."

The medic chuckled, "Oh, I bet you will, handsome. I just bet you will."

Detective Stephen Kaminski had spent twenty-five years with the New York Police Department. With unparalleled instincts and a quick and agile mind, he'd worked his way up from rookie to detective in record time. He'd worked in homicide, a hard unit to survive in as many officers found out after discovering they couldn't handle the blood, gore, and the mental illness that was an inherent part of the cases that landed at their door on a daily and sometimes hourly basis.

He'd had an impeccable record for closing his cases, but after those twenty-five years he'd decided he'd needed a quieter life and a slower pace. He'd wanted away from the mental and emotional drain that was the homicide unit. So, when the opportunity had presented itself, he'd packed up his wife, his teenage children (much to their dismay), and two dogs, and settled down in the sleepy little hamlet of Durbin, West Virginia, a tiny dot on the map in the Allegheny Mountains.

He'd accepted the position of Sheriff with the hope that he'd be able to live his life and perform his duties in an Andy Griffith manner, just a small-town Sheriff with a couple of deputies in a laid-back community where everybody knew everybody.

Trouble didn't happen regularly in and around Durbin, but when it did, it was most often bored teenagers getting a little too loud or drunk on the weekend, or maybe the occasional domestic dispute. It had been a peaceful couple of years, and even though the occasional itch for something meatier, something he could really sink his teeth into, would push at him, he knew, in the long run, he was where he truly wanted to be, doing a job he thoroughly enjoyed.

The shooting on Main Street had given him a boost of adrenalin and piqued his interest. He now wondered just what exactly he'd uncover once his investigation kicked into gear. He'd spoken with some of the bystanders, taken a few statements, and now watched and waited as the two main players were evaluated, bandaged, and given the all-clear by paramedics.

The woman was a nervous wreck. She was absolutely gorgeous, her mass of red hair a fiery halo, and green eyes so vibrant that even the dark of the night couldn't dim their brilliance in the glow of the streetlights. She had classic features, sexy with a touch of country girl. And though he couldn't remember seeing her around town, she looked very familiar to him. Normally he was good with faces and names so he felt certain that he would figure it out. It was just a matter of time.

The man, well, he was a different matter entirely. Military or ex-military – it was written all over him. He was a big guy with an edge, tattoos and piercings, clearly defined, hard-cut muscles. But, Stephen noted, when GI Joe looked at the woman, that edge almost completely disappeared, and his demeanor changed drastically. It was obvious he cared about her a great deal.

Biding his time, he watched and waited until the medics were through with them before walking over and introducing himself.

He raised a hand in greeting. "I'm Sheriff Kaminski."

"Sheriff. Michael Blaisure and Lexi Lane."

"Nice to meet you, but I'm sorry it's under these circumstances. It's not unusual to hear gunshots in these parts, but it doesn't normally happen right here in the middle of town. I'm hoping this was an accident, a misfire, but I'm going to need some more information. How about the two of you fill me in on what happened?"

Blaze wrapped a protective arm around Lexi's waist while he gave his version of the events surrounding the shooting. Stephen noted that he was very detailed and thorough, meticulous in his re-telling, that military training kicking in. "Ms. Lane. Is there anything else you can think of?"

"No, Sheriff. What Blaze told you pretty well covers it. So, what happens now?"

"Well, I've got a few statements to go through and my report to write up. I've got my people, all two of them, out doing some searching trying to see if we can come up with any evidence or find something that would make some sense out of this. We did find the bullet that grazed you and we'll be sending it off to the lab. We've figured out the trajectory of the shot, so maybe once it's daylight, we'll find the casing. Hopefully, when we get everything together and start going through it all we'll be able to piece it together and get some answers. Truthfully? Right now? We're at a loss.

"I'm sure I'll have more questions for you both, but with any luck, we'll get to the bottom of this soon." He took down their contact information and began the short walk back to the station. His mind posed question after question as he walked the quiet streets, but he couldn't seem to find the answers, or at least not any that made sense.

He wasn't certain just how he knew, but some deep-down instinct told him this was just the beginning of a bigger, nastier situation.

The drive back to Lexi's was quiet. So much for the normal he'd spoken of, Blaze thought. He had his ideas about where the bullet had come from but didn't think it was wise to bring it up to Lexi until he had more solid evidence. She definitely wouldn't believe him and would more than likely not want to listen to his speculations.

He parked in her drive, turned the engine off, and stared out the windshield at the cloudless night. Those instincts kicked in again and had him wondering just where the hell they'd been while he'd been getting shot.

Something or someone waited in the dark and his protectiveness went on high alert. He knew she wanted to slow things down but he just didn't think he could leave her knowing that danger lurked, watching and waiting.

"I'm not sure I should be leaving you tonight, Lexi. Actually, there's no question. I can't. I can't leave you knowing you're here by yourself. I need to be here. I'll stay in the guest room, I'll stay out here in my truck, but please don't ask me to leave."

She'd thought long and hard about it on the way home. After the events of the evening, she wasn't quite ready to be alone for the night, either. But was asking him to stay throwing everything she'd said to him earlier in the day right out the damn window? She'd been on the verge of asking him to stay before they'd kissed, but she'd been hesitant, wanting to take that time she'd spoken of to slow things down, to get to know him better. Once he'd kissed her, her hormones had taken over and removed all rational thought.

Then the unthinkable had happened and the sound of that shot had shattered the night. The memory of it reverberated through her mind, echoing through her thoughts in a slow, distorted motion. Her emotions had been all over the place since then. She was scared, she was mad, and she was freaked out that not only had Blaze been hurt, but he'd acted like it was no big deal that he'd been shot. Just another day. She knew that he'd been through hell, but his off-handed demeanor had made it quite clear that they still had so much more to learn about each other.

"I'm not sure you should leave, either." She inhaled and exhaled deeply to have a moment to gather her thoughts, her courage, and then turned to look at him. "Why don't you come inside for a while, and we can talk. We'll see how things go."

She walked in her front door and straight to her wine rack. Choosing a bottle of red at random, she stared at the label as she absently turned it in her hands, thinking, considering, and then promptly put it back. Blaze stood back, arms crossed casually on his chest, and watched in fascination, mildly amused, as she turned to a cabinet and pulled down a bottle of Jack Daniels. When she poured a generous two fingers and downed the burning liquid without hesitating, without wincing, he could do nothing but grin at her.

She poured another shot and started to down it, as well, when she felt his amused eyes on her. When she faced him and offered the shot to him instead, he followed her lead, downing the amber liquid in one swift move. Then before she quite knew what had happened, he had her in his arms, her legs wrapped around his waist, and they were kissing each other senseless.

He came up for air long enough to kiss a trail down the long line of her neck. "Oh, God! So much for talking."

"I need you, Angel. Damn, I've missed you!"

Their urgency for each other became undeniable as he carried her through the living room and up the stairs, stripping her out of her clothes as they went, a telling trail of hot, urgent passion. He laid her on the bed and began ravishing her, tortuous inch by inch. He slowly licked a line down the middle of her body, pausing only long enough to tease each nipple into hard peaks. As he continued, the hot trail his tongue made as it traveled to her center left her panting and wanting.

When she looked down at him and saw him stretched out on his stomach, obviously prepared to stay for a while, the sexy moan that escaped her brought a low growl from deep within his chest. He grabbed her by the hips and pulled her close, angling her body as he prepared to feast. When he claimed her with his mouth, she threw her head back in abandon. She was wet and ready, dripping for him as her arousal trickled from her body. The contrast between his beard and his tongue sent her reeling, intoxicating her with sensation after sensation.

He was in heaven. The sweetness that escaped her only made him hunger for more, and he lapped up the warm honey, savoring each sip. Her clit called to him, begging for attention, and he licked up one side and then the other, tracing it with his tongue and memorizing each tiny detail. Then he sucked the sensitive bundle of nerves into his mouth and teased it until he felt her body begin to tremble in climax. Her legs squeezed together, their involuntary reaction encouraging him to continue to work her over, the knowledge that he'd made her orgasm so intensely making him feel heady with power. More. He wanted more, wanted to give her more.

She was in sensory overload and tried to push him away, to float on the high of her orgasm, but he grabbed her wrists, locking each one in his large, rough hands as he continued to pleasure them both. He never took his mouth off her. Though she tried to resist, to push harder against him, he simply used his forearms and braced against her legs, spreading her further, and opening her wider so that he could dive deeper. She gasped his name as he dominated her body.

He didn't let her come down from her high, and when she realized he had no intention of stopping until she came again, she simply erupted, her overly sensitized clit throbbing as each nerve ending pulsed in pleasure. As she came once more, her mind went blank and stars danced in her field of vision, blinding her with ecstasy.

Breath ragged, she became vaguely aware of movement at the foot of the bed and managed to perch herself on her suddenly released arms. She watched as he stripped out of his T-shirt in a move so slow and sensual it took her breath away. The heavy combat boots he normally wore had been kicked off at some point, though she couldn't remember exactly when. His hard body stood before her and she gazed longingly at his ripped muscles and the amazing tattoos that covered so much of his body. As he lowered the zipper on his jeans and stepped out of them commando, her mouth watered in anticipation.

He grabbed her by her ankles and quickly pulled her to the end of the bed where he kneeled, his hard cock throbbing as the tip leaked his excitement. He covered her with his large body and kissed her lips, building the intensity of the moment with each lick of his tongue into her mouth. Then he slowly eased his cock inside, sheathing himself in her tight heat, and when they were joined, their dual moans of pleasure harmonized as one.

"Lexi," he growled as the intensity stole his breath and her head fell back as she surrendered to the moment, "you are incredible, so perfect." He began to move, relishing each slide into her heat, the grinding of their hips against each other as they met time and again. He pounded in her, long and hard, and she met him thrust for thrust, each giving exquisite pleasure as their bodies moved as one.

It snuck up on him. He wasn't prepared. From one heartbeat to the next, his body shattered. Hot cum shot out of him, the forcefulness of it arching his back before his body stilled in release, stealing his breath. But he wasn't done. More, he had so much more for her, and when he could breathe again, he repositioned them so that she was on her knees. He rubbed his rough palms in circles on her ass as he placed the head of his cock at her entrance. He grabbed her hips and slowly pulled her back against him, expanding and filling her tightness. When he was fully in her, he paused. "I don't want to scare you, Lexi. If I do something, if I frighten you with what I do, I need you to tell me. Promise me you will tell me. I don't want to hurt you, not ever, but I...I need more."

She understood. Somehow, she'd known. She'd known that a man like him would need more than what would be considered normal, vanilla, in the bedroom. She wanted it. She wanted to experience it. She'd been on her own so long, had done it all on her own, made all the decisions for so long and though she needed that control most of the time, she wanted to know what it was like to completely let go. She wanted to know what it was to let someone else, to let him, take full control and submit to him, to his wants and needs. And when she told him, she blew his mind and made his heart race.

"Blaze. Michael. Show me what you need. I promise. I promise."

His life hadn't been his own for years. He'd had his orders, procedures he'd had to follow, directions he'd had to take. When he'd been discharged, he'd finally begun to feel as if he'd gotten his life back, had finally started to take control again. His need to be in authority, to take charge of his life, to dominate, overwhelmed him.

Taking her at her word, he began to move, pulling her hips against him as he pushed inside, slowly gaining speed and intensity. When she felt his hand slap her ass, her muscles constricted, the pain and pleasure mixing deliciously. He slowed his movements as his palm tenderly rubbed the spot he'd just reddened. He continued to fuck her, and once he'd built his speed, he spanked her again, once, twice, three times. Her breath caught and her heartbeat throbbed in time with the pulse of the tenderly abused area on her ass.

More, she wanted more and knew he wanted more. She moaned his name and begged him to take her higher. He pulled her body to his, trapping her arms between their bodies, pressing his chest to her back. His lips went to her neck, kissing, biting, sucking, as his hands went to her breasts. He teased her nipples, gently pinching, and on her gasp of pleasure, pinching harder as he pumped himself forcefully inside her volcanic heat.

Her head rested on his shoulder as her body bowed in pleasure. When his hand snaked up to her throat finding the pressure points on either side of her neck and squeezing gently, her vision wavered, and her body shattered. And when she came, the moans of her ecstasy took him with her into the abyss of euphoria.

She lay on her stomach diagonally across the bed, eyes closed, her body exhausted but replete with all the pleasure they had shared. She felt as if her bones had simply melted, her muscles warm and relaxed. Her mind was a complete blank and she drifted in a hazy sea of sexual fulfillment. Time had lost all meaning. Had it been a matter of minutes, hours, or days? She didn't know and couldn't find it within herself to be concerned.

The bed dipped as he crawled next to her, and her eyes flew open in surprise when she felt the warmth of the wet towel he'd brought with him gently wiping away the remnants of their joining. As he cared for her, he kissed a trail down her spine until he reached her ass. And when he kissed the area he'd reddened with his callused hand, he lingered, showing that he cherished her willingness to explore, to discover, to satisfy their needs.

"Thank you, Angel."

Incredulous she shifted to look at him. "What? Why?"

"I wasn't sure how you would feel about some of the things we did, some of the things I want to do to you, do with you. I mean, we haven't really talked about anything like that. Although, I guess in the grand scheme we haven't really talked about quite a few things."

"I think I should be the one thanking you. I've never experienced anything like that before. It was...wow. Incredible!"

He flashed his crooked grin at her, once again. "Does that mean you might be open to trying other things?"

In answer she crawled on top of him, pushing him down on the bed as she straddled him and kissed him deeply. When she surfaced, she stared longingly into his eyes. "Absolutely."

He rolled, reversing their positions and they spent a very long time doing nothing but kissing languorously, taking their time caressing and exploring each other's bodies. Laughter, whispers, and sexy sighs carried them long into the night.

Chapter Eight

The drive up the mountain had taken the sheriff longer than he'd anticipated. Even after living in the area for a few years, it still surprised him sometimes when the realities of rural living made themselves known. He supposed he'd taken for granted the convenience of a coffee shop or pizza joint on every corner. Urban living meant rarely having to travel more than a few blocks to find what you needed. And while parts of him missed how easily accessible the means to live were in the city, he knew he would never go back. The benefits of less stress, fresh air, and fewer people were, in his book, worth the inconvenience of having to go out of his way to find or do what he needed.

After a late evening preparing reports and doing research, he'd spent the morning with one of his deputies searching the scene of the shooting, combing the area inch by inch. While they hadn't found any new evidence, he had certainly come away from all his work and research with questions he wanted answered.

Lexi Lane. Hot damn, he knew he'd recognized her; knew her name had been familiar. He'd run his search on her and when the once promising country music star's picture and biography had flashed on his screen, he'd been poleaxed.

Country music hadn't really been his thing, but when Lexi had begun to make a name for herself, she'd not only made waves on the country scene, but her sound, rich, pure, sweet, with a hint of twang, had pushed its way into other genres. He smiled sheepishly at the thought that he'd been very attracted to her, had even used a few of her songs to help set the mood with his wife on more than one occasion.

She'd made huge leaps and had been well on her way to mega-stardom when she'd suddenly disappeared from the public eye. At the time he'd thought she'd just burned out like so many in the business do, but after the search he had done the night before, he now knew that had been far from the case.

She'd changed some in the years since she'd left the music scene. She was possibly even more beautiful than she'd been, but there was a sadness there now lurking beneath the surface that hadn't been present during her rising popularity. The story of her life certainly warranted that sadness in his opinion.

Then, of course, there was Michael "Blaze" Blaisure. Now this guy, he thought, was intriguing. The background run he'd done on him had been trickier. A West Virginia native who'd joined the Navy right out of high school. His military file had been suspiciously thin considering he'd been in service for fifteen years. There'd been note of him moving quickly through the ranks, receiving special commendations, and then he'd joined a top-secret special forces unit and the information available in his file had all but dried up until the notation had appeared with his honorable discharge date. Evidently, his time in the special forces had been highly classified.

Both their backgrounds made it quite possible that they could have any number of lunatics looking to cause them harm, or worse. When he'd first gotten the report of the shooting, he'd figured that it had probably been an accident, someone drunk or not paying attention, maybe even someone playing around or showing off to a friend and things getting out of hand; all of which were not too uncommon for the area. Most everyone hunted and even if they didn't, they probably still had a firearm. It was West Virginia, after all.

But everyone they'd canvassed had said the same thing, a single shot followed by total silence. Something about that didn't ring accident or drunken revelry for him.

Now he was on his way up the mountain to talk to Lexi and see if he could put more pieces of the puzzle in place. He could have called to talk to her, but he wasn't ashamed to admit that he wanted another look at her. What hot-blooded male, even one as old and settled as he was, wouldn't?

He found her driveway with no problem and as her home came into view, he marveled at the simple beauty he saw, a true reflection of the property owner. As he parked his truck, he noted something else – a second vehicle. He wouldn't have thought much about it, but the decal, an anchor crossed with the letters USN on the back window, confirmed his suspicions about the owner. Well, well, he thought, two birds-one stone.

Blaze had heard the truck before he'd seen it and hadn't been at all surprised to discover that the driver had been Sheriff Kaminski. Long after Lexi had fallen asleep, he'd lain there going over what he knew, what he suspected, and when he'd risen that morning, he'd done more of his own research, including an in-depth background check on the laid-back sheriff with the Yankee accent. He'd been pleased with what he'd found, his sense of trust rising substantially with his findings.

He had a strong feeling that he and the good sheriff were going to get along well with each other.

He opened the door shirtless and barefoot with his jeans riding low on his hips as the sheriff climbed the deck steps and smiled in greeting over the steam rising from his coffee cup. It wasn't subtle; Blaze's demeanor and actions made it abundantly clear exactly what he was – a protective predator staking his claim on his territory, on his woman, and anything that involved her.

"Sheriff. You're out and about early this morning."

"Old habits die hard. Ya know, getting up early, catching the worm." He paused and looked at Blaze, noting that he seemed to have been expecting the visit. "But I'm guessing that you've already acquainted yourself with me, my background, and my habits."

"Perceptive. And yes, that is exactly how you were described to me – perceptive, intelligent, thorough, and committed. Come on in, Sheriff. The coffee is fresh."

Steaming cups sat in front of them as they settled at the tall counter. "Well, Sheriff. Where do you want to begin?"

An hour later they'd compared notes and posed their questions, and with cautious hesitancy, had stated their suspicions. When Lexi walked into her kitchen, she was surprised to see the two men sitting and talking like old friends as they invaded her cookie jar.

"Good morning, Sheriff."

He nodded his head in greeting. "Ms. Lane. You're looking, ah...rested." He smiled at her and chuckled as he hoped like hell he didn't make her uncomfortable by acknowledging the obvious; she was a woman who'd had her every need met and sexual satisfaction radiated from every pore on her body. "I hope you don't mind me dropping by, but I wanted to follow up and check and see how you, how the both of you, were doing."

When she looked at Blaze and saw his teasing grin, her face flamed, memories of the night before flashing through her mind. "No." She turned her attention back to her guest. "That's fine. Have you found anything or figured anything out?"

"Unfortunately, no. About the only thing I do know with any kind of certainty is that this doesn't appear to have been an accident. If you can answer some questions, it might help fill in some blanks, maybe give me some new leads."

She moved to the coffee pot and poured her own cup as she answered. "Absolutely. I'll help as much as I can, but I've gone over it and over it. I haven't come up with anything that remotely seems consequential."

"Well, to start with," he paused and shook his head, light embarrassment blooming on his cheeks, "hell, I need to go ahead and get this out of the way. I'm a fan. I always wondered what happened, where, and why you disappeared so suddenly. The search I ran last night told me quite a bit. Let me say just how sorry I am for all you went through. You had a miserable hand dealt to you, aces and eights before catching the queen."

"Thank you, Sheriff. And while I understand your poker reference, there's one difference. I walked away from that table when I was dealt that dead man's hand. I survived when everyone else was gone."

"I know it's been a while since you've been on the music scene or had any contact with your fan base, but have you gotten any mail, email, phone calls, that are unusual or threatening?"

"Sheriff, when I left Nashville, then subsequently my childhood home in Kentucky, I did everything I could to completely disappear. I wanted away from everyone and everything. I didn't want to think. I didn't want to feel. The only way to make that happen was to escape and make it appear that I'd simply vanished off the face of the earth.

"There are only a handful of close friends who know where I am or how to reach me. I don't get correspondence or communication from anybody but them, and they'd never betray my location. There shouldn't be any direct records of me being here. I even went above and beyond trying to ensure I couldn't be found. This land was purchased through several layers of shell companies and isn't listed or tied to my name in any way unless someone does a hell of a lot of digging. I do all my business through a company name instead of my own. Other than those close friends I told you about and my attorney, only you, Blaze, and a couple of neighbors even know my full name.

"I even, umm, and I hope I don't get in trouble for this, but I disguised myself for my driver's license picture – wig, colored contacts, and glasses. So, if anyone got into the DMV records it wouldn't be obvious, not by any means, that the Lexi Lane in that picture is me."

He chuckled, "I realized that when I ran you last night. I wasn't going to say anything because I can't possibly imagine what it's like to try to live a normal life when you're a celebrity."

"When I left, I was in a very dark place with no glimmer of light to guide me. I can't say I ever seriously thought about suicide, because that's just not something I would do. But I can say that I teetered on that ledge for a very long time, and it's just been within the past couple of years that I've gotten a safe distance from that ledge." She smiled at Blaze, "And only here recently that I've begun to re-open myself to possibilities." He reached across the counter to her, and she put her hand in his. "I'm not saying it isn't possible, but I just can't see that the shooting last night could have had anything to do with me."

"Well, I intend to keep looking and digging." He checked his watch. "I need to get back, but I'll be in touch. Blaze, I'm going to assume that if I need to talk to you that I can probably find you here."

"I'm not going anywhere until she makes me, Sheriff, and you have my cell number. I don't know if they're after me or Lexi, but, if she'll let me stay, I'm here until we have answers."

When he got to the end of the driveway, he turned in the opposite direction from town and began the trek down the other side of the mountain. It was the long way around to get back to the station, but after his conversation with Blaze, he felt the need to drive by David and Melinda Osborne's house.

Blaze had been full of information. Evidently, his contacts had come through for him sometime in the night and had pulled up some interesting information. It turned out that the friendly, helpful neighbor had served time in the military, too, more specifically, in a bomb diffusion unit within the Army. They'd called him Oz, shortened from his last name, but due to the fact that he was a wizard when it came to diffusing a bomb. He'd been red-flagged a couple of times before being dishonorably discharged for conduct unbecoming a soldier.

More digging had found that those red flags had come from a woman claiming he'd tried to rape her. He'd had a lot of explaining to do and there'd been a lengthy investigation, but ultimately, they'd determined that there'd been a misunderstanding. The Army had chosen to put David through therapy as a course of corrective action in hopes to keep him in service and avoid any further "misunderstandings." But when a second woman appeared several months later claiming rape, he'd been Court-martialed, and the Army had locked him up for a while before they'd sent him packing.

Stephen slowed as he drove past the tiny ranch house. He wasn't sure that Blaze had all his facts straight, but he intended to use his own contacts to verify and find out as much as he could about the Osbornes. One thing was certain, though, Blaze had been on target that something was off about the whole situation. Seeing the house gave him an eerie feeling that he wasn't going to like what he was going to find.

Lexi grabbed the coffee pot and refilled her cup with the dark, steamy liquid then sniffed appreciatively before she took a sip. Blaze watched, noting how even her smallest, most insignificant actions set his body on fire, making him burn with the need to touch, to taste, to devour. When the thought ran through his head that he might never get tired of looking at her, of watching her every move, flutters of panic that he'd thought he'd dealt with bobbed back to the surface.

He'd always prided himself on control, on being able to handle what was thrown at him with a steady hand, but it was becoming glaringly obvious that when it came to Lexi the SOP had been tossed out the window.

"Lexi. We need to talk about last night."

She smiled at him over the rim of her coffee cup. "I really didn't think there was much more to be said. I told you I'm open to new experiences."

He chuckled as he ran a hand over his thick beard. "I fully appreciate that, and yes, actually, before we go much farther than what we did, we really should talk about what we will and won't do and set some boundaries. But that isn't what I was referring to." He paused. "We need to talk about the shooting, Lexi."

"Oh. Alright. I kind of figured out that you and the Sheriff had talked about more than you were telling me."

"Yeah. I asked him if he would let me talk to you first." He hesitated, unsure how to tell her all he'd found about the person claiming to be her friend.

"Just say it, Blaze."

"David-"

"No."

"Lexi, just-"

"No. I can't, I won't believe it."

"Stop. Just hear me out. Please?"

She sighed, "Fine."

She paced nervously as he filled her in on all he'd found and when he'd finished, she sank into the chair next to him, defeated and dismayed. Her mind raced with the information he'd supplied, and sadness that she'd been so easily deceived settled like a lead weight in the pit of her stomach.

"Sheriff Kaminski is going to do his own research so that he can verify what I told him and see if he can unearth anything else, but I don't think he is going to find much more. My guys are pretty thorough."

"But why? Why would David try to harm either of us? He doesn't even know you, and I really have a hard time believing he would want to hurt me. I've been nothing but neighborly and friendly. He has always been very helpful and thoughtful. It, I don't know, it just isn't clicking for me."

"I know. None of this makes any sense and it truly was just a hunch that made me even start looking into his background. I'm sorry, Lexi. I've just had the feeling that something has been off about David from the first moment we met. The situation with his wife, while understandable on one level, is highly unusual.

"Hopefully, we'll get answers soon. Maybe it's nothing. Maybe the shooting has nothing to do with David, but it's at least a starting point, which is more than what we had last night. I guess we'll see what the Sheriff turns up. Until then," he searched her face, "if you're alright with it, I meant what I said, Lexi. I'll stay. I want to stay. I want to be here with you."

It had been an incredibly long time since she'd given in to the need to be with someone, to depend on someone being there for and with her. But she knew, without a doubt, she wanted Blaze to be there, to be someone she could open herself to and depend on, to be someone with whom she could share her thoughts and feelings, for however long their relationship lasted. She crawled in his lap and wrapped her arms around his neck, nodding her head in agreement, and as she laid her head on his shoulder, his arms came around her waist, hugging her close. "Yes. Please stay."

The growl of the lawn mower filled the air as the scent of fresh-cut grass floated on the breeze. Blaze had taken it upon himself to get the push mower out and give it a quick tune-up before tackling the chore of trimming the tall grass and tidying up the already picture-perfect landscape. Though the lawn wasn't overly large, the bright sun shining down on him had caused him to work up a sweat, and halfway through he'd stripped out of his t-shirt, stuffing it in his back pocket where it hung like a white flag of surrender.

He finished up the last strip of the yard and cut the mower engine, pulling his shirt from his pocket and wiping his brow. The quiet that he'd expected to find upon shutting off the mower was instead broken by the hum of an angelic melody. It took him a moment to realize that the sound was coming from Lexi.

Her fiery hair fell in a thick curtain hiding her face as she knelt in the front flower bed pulling weeds and caring for her flowers, lost in the colors, tones, and textures of the bed. He stood and stared at her in awe. The hum of her voice took his breath away. He realized then, that more than anything at that moment, he wanted to hear her beautiful voice flow freely. He needed to hear happiness exude from her in a burst of song that left no doubt about the state of her heart. He desperately wanted, needed to hear her sing.

The quiet of the moment must have gotten through to her and she raised her head to look across to where he stood watching her. The smile that lit her face made his heart stutter in his chest, and he walked over to where she worked and sat on the ground to watch.

"What are you doing, Blaze?"

"Watching you. Listening to you."

The smile slowly left her face. "Listening to me? But I..."

"You were humming. I don't think I can describe just what the sound of your voice does to me."

"I wasn't humming."

"Yes, Lexi. Yes, you were."

"But I can't. I haven't been able to hum or sing, haven't been able to get any kind of music to flow from me since the accident. Nothing, and I do mean absolutely nothing, works. I gave it space, I tried meditation, I tried forcing it, but I haven't been able to sing or play at all. It's been years."

"Maybe it's beginning to come back to you because you were definitely humming. It may just be the start of your music returning, but hopefully, it will come fully back. Hopefully, you will finally heal enough to tap into that part of your creativity, to tap into your soul once more. And I hope with every fiber of my being that I'm around for that day."

"Michael..."

"Just give it time and don't force it."

She looked down at her hands, dirty from digging in the soil, lightly stained from deadheading the blooms past their prime. Her music. She had missed her music almost as much as she'd missed Jackson and her parents. She couldn't help but wonder if he was right. Could it, in some way, be returning to her? Was the wall that had been erected in her despair beginning to crumble? And if it was, maybe the bigger question was, why? Why now?

"You know, I did some soul searching after I left here Lexi. I had quite a bit of time on my hands as I was looking for my land. My time here with you made me realize it was past time that I dealt with all that happened. I found a therapist and began talking things out. As hard as it was to revisit some of those moments, I feel it was one of the best things I could have done. I needed it. One of the suggestions he had was to write out my thoughts and feelings each and every time I had a nightmare. I had reached a point where I would try anything to come to terms with that part of my past, so I gave it a go. When I did, I realized a few things, and I came to some conclusions.

"Sometimes you need the dark to find the light. Sometimes you need the chaos to appreciate the calm. Sometimes you have to crawl to learn how to stand tall. Sometimes you have to lose your ideals to find your truth.

"I've been through the dark. It is miserable and lonely, but I think I've finally started seeing the light. I see that in you and with you. I've lived in chaos, and it almost drove me insane. I'm looking forward to the calm, the calm I find when I'm with you. I've crawled, crawled through some of the most unimaginable situations, lost my bearings, lost my footing, and for all that I went through I feel I can now stand tall - tall and proud. I lost my ideals a long time ago. What I was fighting for changed when I entered the special forces. It morphed into something that made me, the real me, almost unrecognizable.

"Do you want to know when and where I found my truth? I found my truth on a freezing cold, snowy mountain in the middle of West Virginia. I found my truth when I opened my eyes and saw you, Angel."

A solitary tear glistened in the sun as it gently trailed down her cheek. He reached out to her, gently wiping the tear away with his thumb, and she turned her face into his large hand, kissing his palm softly.

"Thank you for sharing that with me. I know what you endured was unimaginable. You seem so different than when you were here in the winter, so much more open. I can tell just how much you've accepted your past, how much you've grown. You may not be at peace yet, but I think you've taken some giant leaps toward the happiness you've been seeking. You're an amazing man, Michael Blaisure."

"Well, I do know one more thing that would make me incredibly happy right now." The gleam in his eyes should have been a warning of things to come, but the flash was so sudden, and he moved so quickly, she didn't have time to react.

One minute she was sitting up, lost in the heart-felt moment they'd just shared, the next she was flat on her back, his large body pressing her down into the soft grass. He claimed her mouth with his own, taking her breath away and making her head spin with the intensity of the kiss. Her arms snaked around his back, her hands smoothing up his large muscles, holding onto him as he ravished.

She felt his erection straining against his jeans as he began grinding against her and the aching that formed between her legs made her moan with longing. He raised up, gripped the hem of the long shirt she wore, and tore it from her body, buttons flying to parts unknown as he ripped it in his haste to get to her skin. Her nipples softly puckered under the pale blue lace that cupped her breasts, called to him. He placed his mouth over the thin material, thrilling her body with the wet heat of his mouth, sucking her in and flicking his tongue quickly. Her nipples tightened into hardened peaks as her arousal soared.

"Blaze. Now. I need you in me now." He grabbed the hem of her shorts and helped her shimmy out of them, then found himself panting as he stared at the blue of her matching thong. A darkened spot, evidence of just how much she wanted him, made him lose his mind with lust. Crazed, he dove for her, lapping at her as he tugged the thin material to the side and slaked his thirst.

The orgasm hit her quickly, rushing through her system and causing her to scream with pleasure. He hurried to unfasten his jeans, the driving need to be inside her pulsing through his body, and when he freed his cock, he entered her quickly, slamming hard into her heat and then holding still as his breath was stolen by the intensity of her fire. Gasping, he looked deep into her eyes and let his feelings for her shine through.

As they began to move, matching each other stroke for stroke, words were said without sound, declarations were made without uttering a word. Their futures, at one point darkened and dimmed, changed forever through tragedy, brightened once again. New hope bloomed, and fate stepped in one more time, changing the course of their lives forever.

In a darkened room a set of hard eyes watched, staring at a bank of screens as the lovers gave their bodies to each other in the warm spring sunshine. Three of the twelve screens offered different angles and views of the couple as their bodies gave and offered pleasure. And as they climaxed for the final time, hate that had started as a slow burn, heightened to a raging inferno.

Blaze's return was an unplanned complication, and the watcher seethed in frustration as they began to reformulate their plans. His return had been unexpected, but the watcher knew that where there was a will, there was a way. And one way or another, they were going to get what they wanted.

Chapter Nine

Sheriff Kaminski reached for his mug and took a sip of his coffee, not realizing that the once steaming hot liquid was now like ice. As the cold, black sludge hit his tongue, he immediately regretted wanting a little extra caffeine to fuel his lagging system. Swallowing the last sip with a wince, he looked longingly at the empty coffee pot and wished that it wasn't his assistant's day off. He'd never once made a decent cup of coffee and today was no different.

He stood and stretched as it finally dawned on him just how long he'd been sitting and staring at page after page of information, his neck and shoulders stiff with tension. He'd reviewed the witness statements over and over. He'd re-read background reports on Blaze, on Lexi. And he'd read and studied the information that Blaze had passed along to him about Lexi's neighbor. He'd used his own contacts and had run his own checks, searching and digging, hoping that he'd find something, anything that would point him in the right direction.

He shook his head, incredulous at just how thorough Blaze and his contacts had been. So far, his own resources hadn't been able to turn up anything more than what Blaze had been able to supply. Maybe, he thought, just maybe it was time to take a trip back up that mountain and have a friendly conversation with David Osborne.

He grabbed his keys and plucked his favored Yankees ball cap off the coat rack as he passed, settling it on his head of thinning hair as he walked out the door and hopped in his truck.

Dust, kicked up by the turn of tires, settled once again as he pulled in the drive and parked his truck. He'd barely made it to the weather-worn covered porch before the door opened and David stepped out, quietly pulling the door closed behind him.

"David Osborne?"

A quick glance around revealed nerves on edge before David met the eyes steadily appraising him.

"Yes, I'm David."

"I'm Sheriff Kaminski. I don't think we've ever been properly introduced."

"What can I do for you, Sheriff?"

"There was an incident in town a couple of nights ago. I really have no leads to go on and I'm making the rounds talking to anyone and everyone who might have been there, or who might have heard anything. I'd like to ask you and your wife a few questions. Maybe you know or heard something that might help."

"I'll be glad to answer your questions, but I'd prefer to not bother my wife right now if that's alright with you. She's resting at the moment, and as she never leaves the house, I don't believe she'd be much help to you."

"I heard that she, that you both, had a hard time a while back. I'm sorry for your loss."

Stress and sadness that had been well hidden suddenly broke the surface of David's features. Lines of worry etched the corners of his eyes, pain and despair revealed the gauntness lying beneath the façade.

"Thank you." He walked to a set of wooden rockers and lowered himself as he motioned for Stephen to join him. The old chair creaked as he settled in the seat and with a slow forward and backward movement, steadily began rocking.

"Well, David, just to clear the air, can you tell me where you were from 6-9:00 on Saturday night?"

"I'm not sure it's much help to you, or that you will even believe me, but I was here. I spent most of Saturday clearing a couple of felled trees. When I got done with that, I worked up at Lexi Lane's house, helping put a roof on her shed. When I finished there, I took a little break and had some dinner. That would have been around 5:30 or so. After that, I came out and started chopping up the trees I'd cleared earlier in the day and storing the wood.

"The nights still get cool, and Melinda, well, she seems to have trouble staying warm enough now. After the trauma of losing the baby, her body just seemed to stop working right, so I try to make her as comfortable as I can." He sighed deeply. "My woodshed is out back. I chopped until it started gettin' dark and the security light came on. I suppose that would have been around 8:30 or so? Can I ask what all this is about?"

"It's funny that you mentioned Lexi Lane as she's part of the reason I'm here. When she was in town Saturday night, she and her companion were shot at."

Surprise had David jumping from his rocker. "Well, shit! Is she alright?"

"Yes, yes. She's fine. She wasn't hurt."

"Whew. Okay. That's good. Wait a minute. Companion? You mean that Blaze guy?"

"Yeah. He took one in the arm. It just grazed him, but he was shot, all the same."

"Well, damn. I hate to hear that. I was a little concerned about him being around Lexi at first, but I've had the chance to talk to him some now and he seems like he has good intentions."

"Yeah, he's a little rough around the edges, but I do believe he plans to take real good care of her. I don't think he's going anywhere any time soon."

"That's good. I never have liked Lexi being on her own up there."

"Do you take this kind of interest in all of your neighbors, David?"

"Sheriff, I'm sure you're aware of my background because you don't strike me as an ignorant man. I never touched those women and if you pull up each and every transcript you will see that my story never changed. I lost my career, and all respect I'd gained for my abilities was thrown out the damn window. I did time for a crime I didn't commit, and I came back here a broken man. My reputation was shit.

"I worked for a long time to put my past behind me. Along the way I met Melinda and she gave me a chance, believed in me when nobody else truly did. We were ecstatic when we found out she was pregnant. I took care of her as best I could. When we lost the baby, when we lost our son, it...it broke her. It broke me. But she needed me, so I quit my job to be here with her full-time.

He cleared his throat before he continued. "Now, no matter what you may think of me, I'm not a stupid man. I'd been putting money aside for years before I was kicked out of the service, and I'd done the same with what I could when I came back here. I saved and I invested. We aren't rich by any means, but we get by well enough.

"As much as I love her, Sheriff, as much as I need and want to be here for her, there are times I just need a break, just need to get out and get some air. Her disease, the depression we both feel, it gets to be too much sometimes.

"I started trying to get to know my neighbors a little better, helping out where I could. I even do an occasional odd job to get a little extra spending money. I know I didn't do anything wrong with those women, and I know we didn't do anything wrong to make us lose the baby, but that doesn't stop me from feeling like I have things to make up for; misplaced guilt can be debilitating. Helping others makes me feel like I'm balancing the scales a little. Does that make any kind of sense to you, Sheriff?"

Stephen took a moment before he answered. "Yeah, I guess I can see what you mean." He stood then and stuck out his hand. "I won't bother your wife - at least not right now, but I may be back again to speak with you both. I appreciate your time."

Stephen began the drive back down the mountain, taking his time and letting his and David's conversation simmer. He couldn't imagine losing a child. The pain and suffering with such a loss had to be unbearable. He could see where going through such a traumatic event could cause a host of mental afflictions.

Though he felt better after speaking with David, there was still something causing him to be wary. Yes, he could definitely see what Blaze had meant about something being off with the whole situation. As far as he was concerned, David was remaining a person of interest until he could get more information or until someone else popped on his radar.

As Stephen rounded a curve, his mind wandering, a shot echoed through the air. His back tire blew out and as he fought for control of his truck, he caught sight of a thin, dark figure rising from a crouch, rifle in hand. Losing the battle for control, his truck went over the edge, crashing through shrubs and thin trees as it rolled down the steep mountainside.

After years of travel and sleeping, or not, in unimaginable conditions, Blaze felt that dozing off in a hammock stretched between two sturdy oak trees in sun-dappled shade was the epitome of relaxation. However, having a beautiful red-headed angel tucked in next to him was absolute perfection, especially as the auburn-haired beauty currently resting peacefully on his chest was the woman that he'd fallen for, head over heels. He'd fallen and fallen quickly. He knew they were good together, and given time, a little understanding and patience, he knew she would see how good they were together, too.

Patience. He'd never had much patience growing up. He'd always been in a hurry to get somewhere, to do something, to learn something. But then he'd joined the military and patience had been drilled into the fabric of his being, along with honor, pride, respect, and love of man and country. In his heart he knew it had taken time, years, to become the man currently contemplating life on a mountainside in West Virginia, but in his mind, it had seemed to happen overnight. Time, he thought, ebbed and flowed in mysterious ways.

He felt himself begin to slide into the dream as his body dropped deeply into sleep.

Alone, they strolled along barefoot, hand-in-hand across a sandy beach, both of them in white, a stark contrast against the rich blue of the sky, the deep teal of the ocean, and the dark brown of the wet sand. Gulls called as they circled and swooped overhead searching for their next meal, while tiny shorebirds ran up and down the beach, playing keep away as they searched for their own meal through the ever-changing motion of the surf.

They were deliriously happy. Lost in the moment, he dragged her to him, kissing her senseless as the cool ocean water rushed in, scurrying around their legs, and burying their feet in the sand in its rush to leave. Their lips parted and he found he was lost once again in the vivid green of her eyes.

The perfection of the moment was shattered as a piercing shot rang out, splintering the peacefulness surrounding them. They looked at each other in confusion then a veil of pain shrouded her eyes, and when a red stain began to bloom on the white material covering her breast, his heart stopped. When she collapsed and her breath began to leave her body, he crushed her slender frame to him and screamed "no" over and over again, begging God or whichever deity would listen to his plight, to return life to her still, cold, shell.

He jerked awake, his heart racing, an agonizing scream ripping through the stillness as he squeezed her to him, overbalancing them and sending them falling to the ground. Blaze landed flat on his back with a thud, Lexi on top of him. Air was forced from his lungs in a rush, a hard punch to the solar plexus.

He barely had his breath back when he rolled her beneath him and began pulling and tugging at her shirt, hands flying frantically to see if she had actually been shot, if his worst nightmare had in fact become reality.

Seeing the panic on his face, Lexi grabbed his hands and began trying to get his attention, to calm him down.

"Blaze! Blaze! Stop! What are you doing?"

She placed her hands on his face and forced him to look into her eyes. "Look at me! Look!"

Gasping for breath, he stared into her vivid green irises, finding them confused but very much alight with life. He took his first easy breath as he finally realized that it had just been a dream, a devastating nightmare. His own eyes closed as he rested his forehead atop hers, his body relaxing degree by degree as he shook off the dregs of the dream.

"Do you want to tell me what that was about?"

"No."

"Really? You almost had a major panic attack, just about mauled me in a desperate search for who knows what, and you think I'm going to let you get by without telling me just what the hell is going on?"

He squeezed his eyes shut in frustration. "No. You're right. I'm not going to keep things from you."

He sat up and pulled her into his lap as he began describing the dream to her. When he reached the point where she'd been shot, she let go of the tears that had been filling her eyes. He watched as they began to track down her face and with a tender touch, wiped them away, one by one.

"I can't. I just can't lose you. Most certainly I can't lose you like that. I swear to you that I'm going to do everything I can to keep you safe, to keep you with me."

"I know. I know you will." She buried her head on his shoulder. "Blaze. I haven't felt this safe, this cared for in so damn long. I still have so much that I'm working through emotionally, but I'm getting there. I've come so far in the short time since I met you. I mean, I'm still afraid. I don't think I could stand to lose someone else that I care about, but I'm happier and more at peace than I've been since the day that Jackson died. That's a good thing, right? A step in the right direction? I need you to do something for me."

"What's that?"

"Promise me you won't do anything stupid, ok?"

"What are you talking about?"

"Promise me that you won't try to confront David on your own."

"Lexi..."

"Promise me."

"Fine. I promise. But I need you to promise me something, too."

"Yeah, yeah. Tit for tat."

"We'll discuss your tits in a minute," he grinned and she smacked his arm playfully, laughing at his light-heartedness, "but right now let's discuss your safety."

"My safety? You're the one who got shot!"

"Yeah, but we still don't know if that was intended for me or if it was intended for you. So, yes, your safety."

"Fine."

"I need to know where you're at, even if you're just going to be working in the yard."

"Alright."

"I don't want you alone with David at any time."

"Alright."

"No going anywhere alone."

"What? No. Absolutely not!"

"Lexi..."

"No. Look, I understand, but I've been on my own for a long time and while I absolutely love having you here, want you here, I still need to have some independence. If I want to go for a drive, or go get my hair done, or just want to go to the damn grocery, I need to be able to do that and do that by myself."

"Damn it."

"We can't be together day and night, Blaze. You need some separation, too."

"Fine. Then I'm putting a tracker on you."

"What? You're kidding!"

"Non-negotiable, Lexi. I need this. I'm crazy enough as it is. If I lost you, I'm not sure I'd survive."

"Ok. What about your safety? You yourself just said we have no idea exactly who that shot was meant for, so how do we keep you safe?"

"Same rules apply. I'll tell you where I'm at or where I'm going, and I'll carry a tracker, too."

"What about David?"

"I can take him."

"Obviously. What I meant was, should we try to be proactive there?"

"You mean, set up some kind of surveillance?"

"I guess so."

"I think we can manage that. I do have a couple of friends that I know I can depend on. I can get in touch with them, maybe get them to come out and see what we can come up with. Maybe get one to set up watch here, one to set up watch around David's? Let me think on it some more."

"Ok. Wow. I'm feeling a little overwhelmed. I've gone from solitude to having you around, which" she smiled at him, "I'm really good with, to possibly having more people around. I'm not sure how I feel about my privacy being invaded like that. It's just a lot to take in."

He hugged her close and buried his face against her neck, taking a moment and breathing in her soft, fragrant scent. "I know these are big changes for you, for me too, for that matter. But if we can figure out who did this and why, maybe we can get past all of this. Then we can slow things down some and take some time to really get to know each other. I know things have happened quickly between us, Lexi, but we're good together, and in time, I think we can be even better together. I can feel it. Can you?"

She took a moment to form her words, to make sure that what she was saying truly reflected her thoughts and feelings. "Blaze. I think we're good together, too. But I need that time. You know, at one point, I had my entire life laid out. I knew exactly who I was, who I was involved with, where my career was going, and where my love life was going. I knew what I thought my final destination would be.

"Don't get me wrong here, I'm good with changes. But changes this big have to happen gradually for me. I can't jump from one situation to the next quite so quickly. I need time to get my brain wrapped around those changes. I need time to adjust. I need time to grow with each step.

"Go ahead and laugh. I know that might seem incongruous with the fact that we spent all of three days together several months ago and now we are all but living together in less than a week. But, Blaze, you never left my mind. Not once during the months we were apart did I go a day without thinking about you. Wondering how you were? If you were still chased by your nightmares? And every day I wondered if I'd ever see you again.

"To an outsider looking in it is going to appear that I'm able to jump from one thing to another in the blink of an eye, but truly, this, us being together, has been building for me for a while now."

He pulled her mouth to his and she simply sank into the kiss. Laying back on the soft grass he continued kissing her as he pulled her on top of him. They lay like that for a while, kissing and caressing, enjoying each other as they took more of those steps to discovery. When they finally came up for air, Blaze spoke first.

"Now. How about we find something fun to do? Want to get that four-wheeler of yours out and go for a ride?"

She grinned innocently at him as she batted her eyes flirtatiously, "I definitely could go for a ride..."

"Oh, I see. You've got jokes." He hugged her close, "I like it! Maybe we can find somewhere while we're out riding, and you can take that other kind of ride."

"Sounds good to me! Hey...why don't I get some stuff together and we'll have a picnic? I know the perfect spot."

"Even better."

Lexi wrapped her arms tightly around his waist as they broke through a dense thicket of trees into a small clearing atop the mountain. She held him closely, not because she was afraid, but because his hard body felt wonderful as she snuggled against his back. At one point during their ride she'd even rested her cheek against his shoulder blade, closed her eyes, and drifted as he'd guided them over and around the bumpy terrain.

They'd taken their time, riding and looking, enjoying the weather and signs of Spring sprinkled along the mountainside. Clusters of wildflowers bloomed here and there, bright spots of color breaking through the brown and green landscape. They'd seen a herd of deer scattering quickly upon their approach, and a pair of foxes had scurried across their path before disappearing into a hollowed-out tree.

Blaze parked the four-wheeler and turned off the power. The absence of the growl of the engine left a stillness in the air which brought a sense of peace and Lexi inhaled deeply as she basked in their surroundings.

"Wow! This is fucking gorgeous!"

Lexi leaned forward and kissed the side of his neck, gently scraping him with her teeth before whispering in his ear, "C'mon. I want to show you something." She jumped off the four-wheeler and had started across the clearing when he grabbed her around the waist and tucked her tightly back against him.

"You really think I'm going to let you get by with turning me on like that and then walking away?" He laughed, "Think again, Angel."

One moment she was laughing as he lowered them to the ground and the next, she was moaning in pleasure as he made her body tremble with desire. He brought her to peak quickly, hot currents rippling through her and making her buck against him as he feasted. But it was when she rode him, head thrown back and body flush with the intensity of her next orgasm that she knew her life had thoroughly and completely changed, once again.

As she looked down at him and saw the warm chocolate of his eyes glaze over as his body stiffened with his own orgasm, his hard cock pulsing hot jets deep inside her, she knew without a doubt she was in love as she'd never been before.

Her heart, once shattered into a million pieces, had somehow forged itself back together, still fragile, but whole and beating once more.

As this realization hit her, she began to wonder exactly what she was going to do about it. Telling him seemed logical, but terror had her holding back. She'd been afraid to let him in, to share herself with him. Now that she had, she worried that sharing the knowledge of her feelings with him would take them further and push her much more quickly than she was prepared to go.

Yes, she knew she loved him, but the thought of taking those next steps left her quaking in fear.

Still connected, she lowered herself onto his chest and rested her head on his shoulder, basking in their loving. His arms held her close, his strength a comfort to her as she relaxed on top of him. She started to speak, but his stomach let loose a loud growl of hunger, making her laugh instead.

"Here I brought a picnic blanket and figured we could have a romantic couple of hours stretched out on it. Instead, we're laying here in the itchy grass, naked as the day we were born, while that blanket sits over there in that basket, unused."

"It's your fault. You started the whole thing. You're insatiable." Playfully, he swatted her ass and made her laugh. "I would say we could dig into that picnic," he paused as a low growl rumbled in his chest and his cock began to stiffen inside her again, "but that's going to have to wait a few more minutes."

"Oh! Well, then. Now who's insatiable? If you think you can hold out..."

His body began to move, his cock sliding slowly in and out of her heat, and she did the only thing she could; she held on tightly as he plunged deep, and they sated their hunger for each other until they both let go, at last.

Chapter Ten

Lexi stood atop her mountain absorbing the same view she'd hiked up to see on the day that Blaze had entered her life. This time, though, he stood behind her, arms wrapped around her, holding her tightly as they savored the view together.

The trees had become denser with the arrival of Spring, filling out where they'd been so sparse during the winter. The air had become warmer and a gentle breeze blew, fluttering her hair about her face. No matter the season, standing where they were and looking out over the mountains and valleys always gave her such pleasure. Now, she thought as she glanced back at him, she had someone to share the view with and it added a whole new layer to her contentment.

No, she was no longer just content, she thought, she was finally, at long last, at peace with her past. And, as much as it made her a bit anxious, for the first time in too many years to count, she was looking forward to her future – to their future and whatever it might bring.

The peacefulness of the moment was broken by the ringing of his cell phone. Blaze answered without looking at the readout.

"Yeah."

"Mr. Blaisure? This is Deputy Shaver. "

"Yes, Deputy. What can I do for you?"

"I just wanted to let you know that there's been an accident. Sheriff Kaminski was up y'all's way earlier this week doing some more investigating into your shooting and his truck went over the edge of the road." Blaze's body went rigid with the news, imagining the sheriff's truck tumbling down the side of the mountain, and had Lexi turning to question what had happened.

"Oh, shit! Is he...How is he?"

"Luckily, he survived. He's in this hospital in the CCU, but it's promising. I've been looking through the files he'd been working on and the best I can tell from his notes, he'd gone up that way to talk to David Osbourne and his wife. We've got a team looking over the scene as well as his truck to see if we can figure out how the wreck happened, but it's probably going to be a few more days before we know anything for sure. With the investigation into your shooting being ongoing, I just wanted to keep you and Ms. Lane in the loop."

"Yeah, uh, thanks. I appreciate you calling and if possible, please let me know if anything changes.

"I'll do what I can."

The call ended and he walked over to a large rock outcropping to lean against it as he took a moment to gather his thoughts. He knew he couldn't keep any of this from Lexi, but the thought of adding more stress to the situation made him leery and cautious.

Curiosity and concern etched her voice. "Well? What's happened?"

Cursing, he exhaled on a huff and began giving her what few details he'd been told. "Lexi. I don't have a good feeling about this."

"Surely it was just an accident. Right?" Worry shadowed her face as her thoughts tossed and tumbled with the possibilities.

"I guess we'll have to wait and see. I don't like it, though. Not one bit." He looked at his watch and did a quick time calculation. "I think maybe we'd better head back down the mountain. I'm calling in my friends, Tank and Viper. I think the sooner they can get here, the better." He reached for her hand, and they began hiking back to the clearing, their moment of tranquility shattered by the horrible news of the wreck.

Steady beeps echoed throughout the room, an audible sensor tracking the rhythm of his heartbeat. The whoosh of a ventilator - air being forced in and out, offset the pulsing of the monitor and set up a strange rhythm. These were the first sounds he heard as his body, broken and bruised, decided to come back online with the world around him.

Sheriff Kaminski blinked slowly as he tried to focus on his surroundings. He recognized where he was immediately. Three white walls and a wall of clear glass combined with the steady hum of personnel moving in the hallway were a clear giveaway, but the antiseptic smell that tickled his nose over and above the oxygen being pumped into him left no doubt.

A nurse in a set of blue scrubs walked in, chart in hand, and seeing his return to wakefulness, began speaking to him as she noted his vitals. He was groggy, in and out of consciousness. Time had no meaning as he floated along on the powerful painkillers that dripped into his veins, liquid relief for the aches and pains that would, no doubt, be unbearable otherwise. One moment the nurse was there, the next she was gone.

It seemed like hours had passed when next he opened his eyes to find the nurse accompanied by a doctor standing over him, one on each side of the hospital bed, and speaking in what sounded like a foreign language. The tubing had been removed from his throat and his mouth was desert dry as he tried to swallow, but he finally felt like he was staying on the side of the living and awake.

As the doctor spoke to him, giving him an update on his injuries, one of his deputies stuck their head in the room to check on him. Once the hospital staff left, his deputy stepped all the way in and pulled up a chair.

"You're lookin' a little rough there, Sheriff. A might bit better than when they brought you in a few days ago, but still rough. You up to filling me in on what you remember?"

His memories were fuzzy and his voice gravelly, but he did what he knew he would want if the roles were reversed, and it was his deputy in the bed instead of him; he started at the beginning. By the time he got to the telling of the accident, he was exhausted.

"I swear I saw someone. I couldn't tell you who as they were camo'd head to toe, but they had a rifle, something for long-range with a scope, if my eyes saw correctly. Leanly built and not overly tall, maybe 5'8" or so? But then, I was looking up the side of the mountain at him so I'm probably off on that estimate. I know the tire blew and that's what sent me into the skid. I don't remember anything after losing control of the truck. Damn it! I haven't had that truck a full year yet."

"I know. That's a damn shame. But the important thing is that you made it out alive. Insurance will cover the replacement of your truck, but we can't replace you." He stood to leave. "And now, I know your lovely wife is pacing the hallways out there so I'm going to go get her and tell her that your ugly mug is still as ugly as ever."

"Thanks. And yeah, you better send her on back here or neither one of us will ever hear the end of her tirade."

He took a deep breath and exhaled sharply as he looked around the room while waiting to see his family. Luck, he thought, had been on his side since the day he'd joined the force all those years ago. Through car and foot chases, shoot-outs and robberies, intense domestic situations, and all manner of other dangers, luck had been sprinkled on his head from a pot of gold. And it was luck, once again, that had saved his ass. Yes, he was lucky, damned lucky to be alive.

Lexi walked into her studio and shutting the door behind her, leaned against it, and closed her eyes. On the promise that she would lock the doors and stay inside, Blaze had driven into town to grab a few things at the hardware store and grocery. He'd told her he was bringing back steaks, even offering to man the grill that evening, and she was looking forward to seeing him show off his manly skills. She'd been giving herself a pep talk from the moment his truck had disappeared from sight.

It was time, she thought, as she opened her eyes. In the few short months since Blaze had entered her life, crashing into her self-imposed seclusion much the same way he had crashed into the side of her mountain, she had felt herself begin to open and feel again. Her heart and mind, her soul, even, had locked down tightly after Jackson and her parents had so tragically passed. Resigned, she had felt there were doors that would never be unlocked again, much less opened with the potential of allowing someone to step through.

But when Blaze had appeared, the lock had vanished, and her heart and soul had cracked open with the tiniest fissure of hope, allowing him to barge in and make himself at home. Now, here she was, her body and mind automatically functioning without daily reminders to breathe, to eat, to live. Her heart, once beating only because it was necessary for survival, had begun fluttering with new love and potential for their future.

Yes, it was definitely time, she thought. She glanced at her piano, took a deep, cautious breath, then forced her legs to carry her over to the stool and tentatively take a seat. She laid her hands on the cover, sliding them reverently across the polished mahogany before slowly raising it to reveal the sleek keys underneath.

Tears threatened to fall as she stared at the ebony and ivory pattern, and her hands trembled with anxiety as she placed them on the keys and cautiously played a C Major chord with her right hand. She gasped and her breath backed up in her lungs as emotions that had been held in check for so long, locked against the world, began to stir inside her. She added her left hand, and when the rich bass line filled out the room, the tear that had formed at the corner of her eye slowly trickled down her cheek.

Something opened inside her and within a few minutes she found herself running through scales with the ease of someone well-practiced. It wasn't long until she was lost in her music, the melodies and harmonies flowing naturally from somewhere deep inside. And when she tentatively added her voice, the room, quietly and patiently waiting as years had passed, filled with audible magic.

That was where Blaze found her two hours later. When he'd returned from his errands, he'd expected to find her outside working the gardens or tending the animals, deliberately disobeying his demand that she stay inside the house until he returned. And when he hadn't found her outdoors, he'd guessed she would be in the living room curled up with a book, or in the kitchen baking up something sweet.

She hadn't been in any of those places. With her nowhere in sight, small flutters of panic had sent him on a search of the rest of the house and to the closed door of her studio.

When he'd heard music, muffled behind the soundproofing layered in the walls, he'd paused in confusion, the sound foreign to him in the normally silent household. Then it had dawned on him exactly what he was hearing and closing his eyes, he stood and listened, basking as her rich alto voice weaved its way through the melody, crossed over into the falsetto of her mezzo-soprano, and fell back into the fullness of her alto. In his mind and to his ears, her voice was perfection, her playing masterful, the combination even more beautiful than he could ever have imagined.

Back when he'd first found out who she was, he'd pulled up some of her recordings and loved what he'd heard. He'd listened to her for hours on end, captivated, adrift in the richness of her sound. There had been something about it that calmed and soothed the beast within him and filled him with hope. But there was no comparison to hearing her voice in person.

Not wanting to disturb her, knowing how incredibly difficult it must have been for her to take the leap and open herself to her music again, he leaned his back against the wall and slowly lowered himself to the floor. He relaxed degree by degree as the song she sang spoke to his soul and calmed the tension that he hadn't realized his body had been harboring.

He closed his eyes and let his mind drift as his body and soul felt...everything.

When Lexi walked out of her studio a little while later, she found him sitting in the hall, head against the wall, his arms resting on his knees, and looking more at peace than she'd ever seen him. She knelt before him and softly placed her hands atop his. When he slowly opened his eyes and began to focus on her, she saw the love and hunger he felt glowing from deep within his soul.

She'd never thought she'd have that deep love given to her again. She'd never thought that she could be open to love again, or that she would ever give that much of herself, that much possession over her heart and soul again, but in that moment, she knew she had given it all to Blaze. Her once-shattered heart welcomed him with open arms and hope for the future.

"Blaze..."

"Lexi?"

"Michael..."

He grinned mischievously at her. "Are you going to use my full name next?"

She laughed softly, "Stop it. I'm trying to be serious here."

"Angel," he took her hand and pressed his lips to the back, "you don't have to say it. I already know."

"Yes, I do have to say it. Maybe I don't have to say it for you, but I most definitely have to, need to, say it for me."

He reached for her face, tracing the soft contours with his rough hands as he cherished the moment she was giving him. "Alright."

"When I lost Jackson, I thought I'd lost my one and only love. I thought I'd lost the capability to love, the potential of a future full of love. Then when I lost my parents, I thought I'd lost everything else. Please don't misunderstand me when I say this. The love I had and still have for Jackson was true love and he will always have a place in my heart. But I only recently realized the truth about that love.

"Our love was first love. It was honest, simple, tender, love, but young and naive. God, I don't think I had any idea just how naive we truly were. I loved him through the dreamy eyes of a teenager our entire short-lived life together. When I think back to all that we'd done together, shared together, I can see the stars sparkling in our eyes. We were blinded by those stars. What I used to think of as the perfect relationship, I now see for what it truly was.

"You see, it was never a true partnership between us. I have no doubt that he loved me, but he, and this is going to sound odd, but he gave me everything I ever wanted. Yeah, that sounds weird. He catered to my wants and whims. It was almost as if he was afraid that if he didn't give me everything I asked for, I would leave him.

"I told him I wanted to sing? He took it upon himself to find me places to sing. I told him I wanted to move to Nashville? He found us a house, hired a moving company, and two weeks later I was living in Nashville. I told him the record company wanted me to go on tour? He almost pushed me out the door to get me on the plane, knowing that it was what I wanted and had wanted for a long time.

"Maybe that kind of devotion is what some women want, and at the time I didn't see it for what it was, but now I know. He wanted to give me a fairytale happy ever after and I will cherish him for that and hold him in a special place in my heart forever. But I can honestly say that if he'd lived, if we'd actually gotten married and had that family, my dreams and aspirations at the time would have swallowed him whole, leaving nothing of the man he was truly meant to be.

'You know, I don't think I ever actually asked him what he wanted from his life, from our life together. He certainly never told me what he wanted. He was so content with pleasing me that he never even offered that part of himself to me. His world revolved around giving me everything I wanted and what he thought I wanted before I even had a chance to voice those wants. Knowing Jackson, if I'd asked what he wanted, what he needed from life, he would have simply said that his only want was to see me happy. I was too blinded by the romance of it all to see the writing on the wall.

"I didn't know how much I needed someone like you. Someone to be a little stubborn with me, and to make me realize that a truly loving relationship encompasses the wants and needs of both parties. I didn't know how much I needed someone to love me who would also be able to stand up to me, to stand up for themselves. I didn't know love, deep, passionate, heart and soul love until you came into my life.

"Blaze, I've been through the dark and after a very long time, I found the light, but you brought my sunshine. I've lived in chaos and have searched for and welcomed the calm, but you've brought my peace. I've crawled until my hands and knees bled in my efforts to stand tall, but it wasn't until you came into my life that I was able to rise above. I lost my ideals through tragedy and lived in a world of half-truths, but when you crashed into my mountain, into my life, my existence once again had authenticity.

"You've given me what I thought I would never want again, what I thought I would never get the opportunity to experience. You've opened my heart and helped me to believe once again in possibilities. Michael...you've given me yourself, your struggles, your joys, your hopes and fears, and in the process, you've given me more than

I ever dreamed would be within my reach again. You did it. You brought back my music. With you, I feel whole once more. With you, I'm open to love once more."

"Lexi..."

"Shh..." She placed her finger on his lips to stop him. "I don't need the words, Michael." She stood up and held her hand out to him. "Show me. Just show me. Kiss me, touch me, fill me, let me feel your love. Let me give you my love in return."

He took the hand she offered and when he was standing in front of her, kissed her with everything he had, giving her all of himself, all his love in the simplicity of the kiss. When her body was a puddle in his arms, limp from passion and longing, he scooped her up and carried her to the bedroom.

Late afternoon sunlight filtered through the filmy curtains in the bedroom, softening the room into shades of gray relieved only by a beacon of golden light as the sun shone down through the skylight and onto the bed. He sat on the edge of the mattress and settled Lexi on his lap. Their kisses, loving declarations of their feelings, made them ache with want, made them shiver in anticipation. Their bodies hungered for more, and though they hungered they held back, relishing and drawing out the intensity of the moment.

They undressed each other, touching and tasting as they went, and when they lay facing each other on the bed they began a tender exploration of each other's bodies. Gentle caresses made their skin tingle as soft sighs, moans, and gasps of pleasure reverberated through the air. When he lay atop her, cradling her in his strong arms, they looked deeply into each other's eyes, steeped in the moment, in each other.

And as he entered her, they voiced their love for one another, sharing the most precious of moments, a turning point away from the heartbreak of their pasts. Two hearts united, two souls intertwined, two bodies connected, and destinies aligned.

Chapter Eleven

Lexi chuckled as she lit the last of the tiki torches on the back deck. "Are you sure you don't want me to give you a hand?" The night was warm, and a soft breeze blew from the south gently rustling through the trees. Fireflies danced across the lawn, crickets chirped in the distance, and a Great Horned Owl hooted nearby, night music serenading them as the fire crackled on the grill.

"Nope! I told you. I've got this."

"Are you sure? Because I'd prefer my steak grilled, not charred to a crisp."

"Think you're funny, don't ya?"

"Well, you might need to turn the heat down on the grill or neither of us is going to be laughing. Then again, you may very well singe your eyebrows with the flames that high and then I'll be laughing my ass off."

"Yeah, yeah. Why don't you just sit that adorable ass of yours down and relax? I told you I was taking care of dinner tonight. I don't want you to do anything but sit back, prop your feet up, drink your wine, and watch me work my magic."

"I thought I'd already gotten a first-hand magic show?"

"Oh, but I have so many more tricks up my sleeve." He walked to her and braced himself on the arms of the chair where she reclined and leaned in to kiss her, stopping a hair's breadth from touching her, their lips almost but not quite meeting. Her soft gasp made him grin and with heat in his eyes he licked her, tracing her full lips in a sensual tease that made her squirm with anticipation as her arousal scented the air.

He pulled back and stood looking down at her, searing her with his stare, and when his gaze roamed down her body, he found her nipples pebbled hard and puckering underneath the thin white material of the tank top she wore. His head fell back as a low growl rumbled deep in his chest.

When he glanced back down at her and adjusted himself, she couldn't help but giggle. "You know you brought that on yourself, don't you?"

He looked down at his cock as it strained against the material of his jeans, throbbing with need. "It was worth it." Then he grabbed himself and gave her a smoldering look, "Or, it will be worth it very, very soon." His eyebrows raised, a sexy invitation for the night ahead, and he chuckled as he turned back to the grill.

"I've got something for you, Lexi." Blaze reached into his pocket and pulled out a gold bracelet. Dainty links caught the shimmer of the tiki torches as he held it out to her. A music note, black outlined in gold dangled from the center of the chain and Lexi stared at it in happy confusion.

"What's this for?"

"Well, I told you I wanted you to carry a tracker. It was delivered today – another reason that I made the trip to town. I wanted to get it and get it on you as soon as possible."

"It's beautiful!"

"Well, even though it's a tracker, I wanted it to be something that you might actually like."

"I do, I really do." She held out her wrist and he fastened it in place, kissing the back of her hand once it was secure.

"I've loaded the tracking app on my phone, and I've already sync'd the bracelet to it. My tracker came, too and I'll load that on your phone once we're done here and I'll show you how it works."

"Blaze. Thank you."

"Just make sure you wear it. That's all the thanks I need."

They were just finishing a bottle of wine and preparing to clean up when a soft whistle got Blaze's attention. It repeated, a code that had Blaze instantly on high alert.

His friends had arrived the day before and after introductions had been made, they had disappeared, each with their assignments, each intent on keeping Lexi and Blaze safe and aware of any unusual happenings around the property. The signal one of them had sent had Blaze calmly but quickly going into action.

"How about you go on inside, Lexi? I'll clean up and join you in just a minute."

The urgency in his voice might have been missed by anyone else, but she had learned to recognize the subtle tones and changes in him in a short period of time. She got up, grabbed her glass of wine, and walked through the back door that he held open for her. She turned to question him and saw that he'd pulled out a pistol she'd been unaware he carried, and the mild panic she'd felt began to amplify.

He closed the door quietly and was gone before she could say anything further.

Gun hidden at his side, Blaze walked to each tiki torch and extinguished their flames. One by one the lights inside the house were turned off, just another indicator to him of Lexi's intelligence. In total darkness, he inched his way off the back deck and to the corner of the house. He paused and listened, inched some more, paused, and listened again.

He caught the sound of footsteps as they lightly jogged across the back edge of the lawn and knew it wasn't one of his guys. His guys were lethal and trained to be silent in their deadliness. His eyes began to adjust to the dark and caught the outline of a figure as it disappeared into the dense branches of the pines that marked the property.

He gave chase and had just entered the thick foliage himself when a shot rang out. The footsteps he'd heard got louder before they eventually faded leaving him mad and frustrated that he hadn't caught the intruder. He pulled out his phone and did a quick check-in with his friends as he walked back to the house.

He wasn't prepared to step up on the deck and find Lexi waiting, her own pistol at her side. The image of her standing there prepared to defend herself, her home, and the man she loved, painted a sexy picture in his mind. But seeing the nerves beneath the sexy confidence she exuded stopped him in his tracks.

He wasn't certain how he could have forgotten just how stubborn and independent she could be, but the panicked frustration that had begun to rise in him at finding her outside the house faded quickly when she wrapped her arms around him. She held on as if her life depended on it, her body shaking in relief, and he gathered her close to calm them both.

"I thought you understood you needed to stay inside, Lexi."

"I know but I couldn't. I couldn't let you face whoever this is without me. I won't hide and I won't be a prisoner in my own home."

"I'm sorry. I know this must be hell for you, but I can't lose you. Please just trust me, trust my friends. We aren't going to let anything happen to you."

"Yeah, well, I can't lose you either, Blaze. I can't go through something like that again."

With that, the last of his frustration disappeared, air fizzling out of an untied balloon. "I know, Angel. I know." His phone dinged with an incoming message. One look at the readout had him cursing as he quickly typed out a reply. "Lost him. Whoever it was had an ATV hidden about a mile from here. Damn it!"

He walked to the edge of the porch and leaned on the wooden railing as he contemplated the situation. Lexi joined him and snuggled against his side. "Well, there's good news and bad news. The good news is that he knows we are aware and are taking precautions. The bad news is that he knows we are aware and taking precautions – we've lost the element of surprise. My guys will re-position, but whoever this is will be more alert, and maybe even more on edge next time."

"Maybe it will scare him off and there won't be a next time?"

"Lexi. I love your optimism, but we were shot at, I took a bullet, Sheriff Kaminski was shot at, wrecked his car, and almost died. I don't think this guy is going to scare that easily."

"What are we going to do?"

"Well, I've been giving that some thought. The way I see it, we can continue to sit and wait and hope that the police turn up something, or we can try to take care of this ourselves."

"What exactly do you mean by us taking care of it?"

"I contacted my friends because I wanted protection for you. But maybe we need to take it a step further. Maybe we need to try to set a trap?"

"A trap? What kind of trap?"

"I'm not sure yet, Lexi." He wrapped his arms around her waist and pulled her tightly into a hug. "Let me think on it a bit and I'll see what I can come up with. I'm just extremely tired of sitting and waiting for whatever this asshole is going to do next. I don't want us to have to keep looking over our shoulders worrying about what else he has up his sleeve.

"You should be able to go in your own yard without having to be constantly looking over your shoulder for danger. You should be able to have a nice dinner under the stars without being spied on. You should be able to be naked on this porch gripping this railing like your life depended on it with me fucking your brains out from behind until you scream that I am Lord and master of your body as you orgasm, and your pussy spasms, squeezing my cock in a hot vice grip until I blast you with my cum.

"Instead, the house is now under 24/7 surveillance, and as much as I love Tank and Viper, and would trust them not only with my life but your life - which is so much more important to me - I'm not into putting on a show for them."

"Wow." She giggled. "That escalated quickly."

"Yeah, that isn't the only thing that escalated quickly." He reached between them and adjusted the bulge straining against his jeans. "You didn't put a bra on tonight and the breeze has picked up enough that it's gotten a little chilly. Your nipples are rock hard, and I can feel them poking against my chest. Their attention kind of got my attention."

"Well, we may not be able to be naked on the back porch right now, but we can certainly get naked anywhere we want inside the house. I could use a nice soak in the tub. If you join me, I promise that I'll show you just how dirty getting clean can be. I can guarantee that I'll make every moment of it worth your while."

"Spending time naked and wet with you is something that you'll never have to sell me on, Angel."

She laughed loudly when he scooped her up, put her over his shoulder in a fireman's hold, and carried her in the house and straight upstairs.

"What would you say if I told you that I want to take you away from here for a while?" Steam from the hot water hung in heavy droplets throughout the bathroom. Candlelight flickered from votives scattered around the tub and pillar candles dotted around the room. Lexi drifted as she leaned her back against his massive chest, her body snuggling against his as he surrounded her. She rested her head on his shoulder as his hands, his magic, thrill-inducing hands, massaged and teased her body relentlessly.

He kissed her neck as his thumbs brushed across her nipples, arousing her body further than she'd ever thought possible from such a simple touch. And when her breath backed up in her lungs with a soft gasp, he growled, the animal inside him scenting his prey. The ache he'd caused deep inside her reached new heights as arousal swamped her with need.

"I say, I can't think clearly when you're making me feel this way."

"Well, then don't think. Just tell me what your first instinct was when I asked you."

Reluctantly, she slid out of his embrace and stared down into the water. "It's not that easy, Blaze."

"It can be. I can be just that simple. Trust your instincts."

She turned then, maneuvering herself so that she faced him, straddling his lap, linking her arms around his neck as she looked into his eyes, at the unconditional love she saw reflected there. "As much as I would enjoy getting away with you, as much as I look forward to taking those steps with you, I won't, I absolutely refuse, to be chased away from my home, my sanctuary, because some asshole is out wreaking havoc on my life and the lives of those around me.

"I mean, we don't even know for sure if all of this is because of me, or you, or if this person is just clinically insane. I want answers; I need answers. Yes, I want to go away with you, but I can't do that until there is some sort of resolution to all of this. When I go away with you, I want to do so knowing that all of this is behind us and that when we come back, we can come back to peace. Does that make sense to you?"

She'd piled her hair atop her head as they'd gotten in the tub and loose tendrils had begun to escape, curling madly in the wet heat of the bathroom. He tucked a strand behind her ear before framing her face with his hands and caressing her cheek with his thumb. He searched her eyes, her face, and knew that even though it wasn't the answer he'd hoped for, it was the answer he'd expected.

He knew that though there had been a time in her life where she'd been content to run, where she'd seen no choice but to hide, things had changed. Good or bad, what he wanted or didn't, the woman before him would never again give in to the bullying that life sometimes gave. Now, she would stand. She would fight. She would conquer.

"Alright. We'll get through this. We'll get through this here, on your mountain. We'll get through this together."

"Thank you."

"Just know that when this is all over, when this person is behind bars and we can breathe easy again, I'm taking you away on a vacation that you will never forget, that we'll never forget."

"I like the sound of that. So, where exactly are we whisking off to on this grand adventure?"

"Oh, I have several places in mind that I want to take you. Places to wander aimlessly, to sightsee, to rest and relax in the sun, but I think the first place, our first trip together, will be a surprise. You see, Lexi, I plan on us taking our time traveling to all these destinations. I plan on spending years and years making sure that we go, do, and see all the things we want. Lexi, I plan on spending the rest of my life having these experiences with you."

Her body froze and the slightest look of panic crossed her face. "Michael-"

"Shh..." He pressed a finger to her lips. "Don't. I'm not asking." He grinned, a mischievous look gleaming in his eyes, "Not quite yet." Tension that had suddenly built began to slowly ease from her body. "But one of these days I am going to ask and Lexi, there's only one answer I'm going to accept. I'm not letting go of you, not ever."

Unsure of what to say to him, knowing that though she loved him she wasn't quite ready to take that next leap, she did the only thing she felt she could at that moment. She kissed him. Their lips met time and again, their breaths mingled, their tongues teased and tasted, and their kisses held promises, not only for the intimacy of the night to come, but for the future they both knew lay ahead of them.

Seething in anger, a lone figure sat in the dark staring once again at the bank of monitors. Wild thoughts swirled in a demented mind. Derogatory slurs were hurled at the screens, at the wall of snapshots, headshots, and clippings of articles that covered one wall of the dingy room.

On another wall, a whiteboard resided with a list, carefully thought-out steps to achieve a desired outcome. Steps one and two had been checked off the list – completion visualized. Step three, however, had been written, crossed out, and re-written several times – a listing of obstacles and challenges as they'd arisen.

Yes, the figure thought, step three was proving to be a bigger challenge than originally planned. But given time and the right set of circumstances, even step three would be completed. Once that obstacle was out of the way, there would be no stopping them from getting what they wanted.

There would be no stopping them from getting all they felt they deserved.

Chapter Twelve

The wind caught the heavy glass door and clipped his bad shoulder, causing him to curse as he hobbled into the police station and over to his desk. It had been a full week since he'd been released from the hospital and Sheriff Kaminski could no longer stand to be laid up in bed being waited on hand and foot.

He loved his wife and family, but their hovering had just about driven him insane. He'd needed out of the house, he'd needed to check on his station, his employees, his cases, and even though the atmosphere wasn't what one would call restful, it was exactly the kind of rest that the doctor had called for. Well, if you considered him the doctor, that is.

His assistant walked over to him, full coffee cup in hand, and stared disapprovingly at him as he gingerly lowered his aching body into his desk chair. The cracked red leather had seen better days, but the foundation of the chair was solid, and in his mind, the foundation, no matter what you were talking about, was the most important thing. A solid foundation could withstand most anything that threatened.

He knew that the solid foundation he and his wife shared had made it possible for them to weather many storms over the years. Just like he knew that a solid foundation of police work was what withstood the hills and valleys, the twists and turns, and the metaphorical, and sometimes even literal, bombs that were occasionally dropped on an investigation.

He took the coffee cup, thanked his assistant, and had just fired up his computer to begin updating his notes on the Lane/Blaisure case when his deputy walked in and sat in the visitor's chair on the opposite side of his desk. Hat in hand his deputy crossed his ankle on his knee and looked questionably across the desk at him, no doubt taking in the black and blue bruises that still ranged across his face and smirking at him as he shook his head in disbelief.

"Sheriff."

"Deputy."

"Pushin' things a might bit, ain't ya, Sheriff?"

"Maybe by some people's standards."

"But not by your standards, huh?"

"Nope. I'm good. I'm ready to get back at it. Ready and raring."

"Couldn't take another minute of being waited on hand and foot?"

"Dear God, no! If one more person offered to help me get to the damn bathroom just so I could take a piss, I was going to lose my fucking mind."

They both chuckled.

"Alright, Deputy. Fill me in."

"Sure thing, Sheriff. Got a call from Blaisure yesterday morning. Seems they had unwanted company a couple of nights ago. Nothing really happened and whoever it was got wise to the fact that they'd been discovered. Took off. Blaisure gave chase but it seems they had means to get away stashed a little way from the house. They jumped on a 4-wheeler and were gone before anyone could get a look.

"Also, Blaisure came clean that he has a couple of buddies staked out up there keeping an eye on things. Supposedly they're just there for surveillance, but from the way he talked, if it came right down to it, they would protect and defend by whatever means necessary. I had a nice long chat with him about vigilante justice and gave him and Ms. Lane some warnings.

"At this point, there isn't much more we can do about that. He's smart. And I have a feeling the men he has up there are just as smart. But you know as well as I do that

Blaisure is also deadly as fuck, which means his friends are probably just like him.

"From the standpoint of an American looking toward our military to serve and protect, I'm glad we have people like him. But he hasn't been out long, and I don't know how quickly or how well he's adjusted to civilian life. I guess we'll see."

"Thanks, Deputy. I had a feeling he was going to do something, but I wasn't sure what it would be. I think you're right that he'll be smart about it, though. We just have to hope that his protectiveness doesn't outweigh the smart. Do you feel I need to have another talk with him?"

"Nah, he gets it. I think he's just worried about Ms. Lane. I can't blame him. Shew! She sure is a mighty fine woman."

"I've got eyes, Deputy, and they didn't get injured in that wreck so I can say with absolute certainty that I agree 100%. She's a looker. Any news from the lab about my wreck?"

"Yeah, I updated the file, but pretty much you were correct. Your tire was shot out by a .308 Winchester. Ballistics is saying that it will probably match up with a Remington 700. If we can get our hands on the gun, it should be an easy match. When the tire blew it sent you into a spin. You hit the curve up there wrong, and the combination of that and the gravel road sent you over the edge. You were lucky that the damn truck didn't blow up, lucky that we got to you when we did, but you were even luckier that the person who reported the wreck was coming up the mountain and caught sight of you as you flipped."

"Thank God. There's no telling how long I would have been there otherwise. Thanks for doing all the follow-up. I think I'm going to sit here and go back through the file, let things sit and simmer in my brain for a bit. Hopefully, something will click, and we can finally get somewhere on closing down this case."

"Sure thing, Sheriff. I think I'll take me a quick walk around town, stretch my legs a little, make sure that everything's nice and quiet out there, then I may do the same."

"You do that. Then you can bring me back a piece of Ma's chocolate cake when you're done flirting over at the diner."

"Me? Flirtin'? Now, what on earth would give you a crazy thought like that?" Stephen looked at his deputy and shook his head, chuckling as the baby-faced officer winked before sauntering out the door.

There was a time, Stephen thought, that he'd have done the same thing. He looked at the pictures of his family sitting on the corner of his desk and smiled. Yeah, there was a time, he thought. But he sure was glad that he'd found the beautiful, strong woman that he'd spent the past 18 years with. She might drive him a bit crazy with her worrying sometimes, but she'd sure made his life brighter just by being in it. And he knew beyond a shadow of a doubt that she'd do anything for him, for their kids.

With that thought, his mind began to wander, and wandering he began to work his way through the file from the beginning, going through it step by step, detail by detail.

Late that night as Blaze and Lexi lay in bed, her spooning him, arms and legs tangled together in a happy jumble, Lexi sighed contentedly and placed soft kisses along his neck and up to his ear. She couldn't remember the last time she'd been so happy. Enjoying the moment, she laid back and snuggled into her pillow. She had just begun to drift off to sleep when Blaze asked the question she'd been wrestling with since the day she'd finally broken through the barrier blocking her from her music.

"Do you think you would ever want to get back into the music scene? Record? Travel? Perform?"

She lay there for several minutes before she answered. The thoughts had been there from the very first note she'd played. Could she do it? Would she want to? She still wasn't certain.

"Honestly, I don't know." Disentangling herself from his body, she rolled to her other side and stared out the bay window at the stars dotting the dark sky. She felt the bed shift and his strong arms wrap around her, his body curling, protecting, and reassuring her, letting her know without words that he would be there for her no matter her decision.

"I've never given it much thought. Mostly because I had assumed that part of me was gone forever. I mean, why think about, worry about, something that is no longer attainable, right? Maybe somewhere in the back of my mind I thought that if I got the chance I would do it, that I would pursue that again. Now? I just don't know.

"Having that part of me returned is so precious and I will never take it for granted. Am I up to sharing that with anyone other than you? At this point, no. I don't think so. It's still too fresh, too much on the surface. Maybe, just maybe, one of these days I will decide to take that step. Not now, though."

"It's your decision and I will support you either way. But I need you to know this, Lexi, I'm not Jackson. If you make the choice to go back on the road, I'm not going to be content to put you on a plane and wave goodbye from the tarmac. No, if you make that decision, I'll be with you every step. I'll be by your side all the way. I'll stand in the wings and watch you perform every night.

I'll camp out on the sofa in the studio while you record. One way or another, we'll be together. You see...it's no longer just you. Now, there's us."

She smiled as she let the word roll around in her mind. Us. "I love the sound of that."

"Yeah, Angel. I do, too."

"So now it's my turn for a question."

"Shoot."

"Really?" Her eyebrow raised, questioningly. "Shoot? With us in the situation we're in, 'shoot' is your choice of verbiage?"

He laughed, "Fair point. Alright, ask your question."

"Well, we've established that we're together, that we're going to be together. You're living here, at least for now. And if I get my way, forever." She leaned in and kissed him tenderly.

"I haven't heard a question yet, Lexi."

"I guess that's my question. Stay. Will you stay? I know you have your land and plans, and I know you wanted your own. But will you just stay here? With me? Make new plans and dreams here with me?"

"Lexi. You humble me. I don't think I ever told you that when I first saw this house, I wanted it."

"You wanted my house?" She grinned as she teased.

"Yes. The snow was coming down like crazy, and my defrost and windshield wipers were working hard to keep my view clear. And I looked up your driveway, up the mountain, and there it was. It was like a homing beacon to me. I just didn't know then that it truly was where I was meant to be. I didn't know that your house was my final destination. I didn't know that my home was waiting here for me. You, Lexi. You're my home. No matter where we live, as long as I'm with you, I'm home."

"Michael..."

"So, yes. I'll stay. I'm here and I'm not going anywhere. My plan was to build but building a life with you, no matter where we are, is all I need."

Happy and content, they snuggled closer, and tangled together, drifted to sleep.

Lexi woke early and went about her morning chores as if it were any other day. She'd left Blaze sleeping soundly in bed, his muscular body stretched out on his stomach, his naked ass tempting her to simply crawl back in beside him and take a bite. Though she paused more than once as she seriously considered the possibilities, she continued to slip on her clothing, and quietly crept through the house and out the front door to care for the animals.

Standing on the deck she took a moment to appreciate all she'd done; all she'd built and created for herself in the years she'd been there. She thought of Blaze and all he'd brought to her life in the brief time he'd been around.

She smiled and warmth spread through her when she thought of the protectiveness that Blaze had shown from the very beginning, the protectiveness he continued to display. In her mind, he was the epitome of an alpha male and it thrilled her that she was the one he chose to shield and protect, to love and to cherish. She'd never known how freeing it could be to drop her guard and let go of the reins. With Jackson, everything had been different. He'd loved and cared for her, but he'd never been the protective type. And while she could appreciate the fact that Jackson had let her be her own woman, the exciting yet peaceful cocoon of Blaze's love was where she felt she was truly meant to be – where she'd been meant to be all along.

And while there was nowhere she wanted to be more than with Blaze, she was finding she needed some time, even if it were only a few moments, for herself, by herself. She enjoyed his company and wouldn't have it any other way, but ever since the most recent incident, he'd been hovering. Protective and cared for she wanted; hovering she could do without.

A week had passed and during that time he'd never left her side for more than a few minutes other than his trip to town, and while she appreciated his concern and his need to keep her safe, she was beginning to feel as if she were smothering. Obviously, they were going to have to work on finding balance. Somehow, some way, they needed to ensure each other's safety while retaining their freedom. They needed to enjoy each other's company and presence while still having the ability to step back and let each other grow and bloom.

She was extraordinarily happy to have him be a part of her life, to be close by, but she'd spent many years in forced independency. Having done it all on her own for so long, it was hard to remember to lean on him, that she could lean on him. She knew that he worried, and with good reason. But going from living such a solitary life for so long to suddenly having someone else around, she'd come to realize that she missed some of her alone time and its advantages.

With those thoughts floating through her mind, she walked toward the sideyard to relish the peacefulness of the morning and carve out some of that much-needed time for herself, even if it was only long enough to mark a few chores off the daily list.

With bucket in hand, she made her way into the chicken coop and began spreading feed, the familiarity of the chore left her feeling calm and at peace. She grinned as the chickens surrounded her, happily pecking at her offerings. And as the chickens ate, she began to hum. Soon, her humming turned to words, her words into a song.

When the realization of what she'd done hit her, her heart began to thud, her mind began to whirl, and disbelief stopped her in her tracks.

Dreaming again. He knew and recognized it as such, but as this dream made him not only happy, but horny, he went with it and enjoyed the ride. The haze that shrouded the dream hung over his vision like a filmy curtain, but he could see through it to the endless surprises that the firecracker he'd fallen in love with continued to heap on him.

He was lightly dozing on the couch when she appeared in front of him, her magnificent body bound in black leather, thigh-high stockings secured by a garter belt, black stilettos giving her already long, sinuous legs the appearance of even more length to get tangled in. Seeing her caused him to instantly wake and his cock to nearly burst with the speed that it hardened. She crooked a finger at him, and he jumped to follow her like a puppy being offered a special treat.

Up the stairs they went, him watching the perfect roundness of her ass as she climbed each step slowly, tempting and teasing him. When they reached the top of the stairs she didn't go to their bedroom. Instead, she continued down the hall to the guest room, the room he'd used those couple of nights when they'd first met.

She paused at the door and looked over her shoulder at him, taunting him with a sultry look, teasing him as she flirted. He itched to touch her but each time he reached for her she inched away, keeping him just out of reach and making him want her even more for her playfulness. Then she opened the door and they stepped into what he considered a playroom, a wonderland to fulfill his every sexual need and desire.

Had he fallen for the Little Mermaid? Gadgets and gizmos aplenty! He grabbed her then as primal lust ravaged his body with need. Cuffs and chains dangled from a wall and that ravenous hunger had him sandwiching her body against it. He chained her, arms and legs, and when there was no escape for her, when she had no choice but to give in to his wants, his needs, then and only then did he do what he'd wanted to do from the moment he'd wakened to find her in front of him. On the floor, on his knees, he yanked the thin strip of leather from between her legs and greedily ate the feast she offered while a long, low growl vibrated from deep within his chest.

His heart hammered, growing steadily louder, more impatient... He couldn't stop. Her taste? So sweet! Her warmth? My God, her heat! Her clit? A perfect bud that he wanted to spend the rest of his life licking and savoring! His cock throbbed with the need for release...

He felt himself slide out of the dream and into the reality of Lexi and her naked body straddling him. Her breasts pressed against his abdomen; his arms trapped against his sides by the silky smoothness of her thighs. His body was on fire as he felt her warm lips sucking him into her mouth, her tongue licking him and sucking him down her throat.

He gasped as his eyes flew open and were met with the luscious sight of her ass bared to him, glistening with arousal, sweet nectar that he had no choice but to lap up. Dream and reality merged, and he buried his face in her pussy. His tongue swirled and licked, and he swore, absolutely swore, he could feel her heartbeat in her clit. She throbbed for him, and it made him delirious.

His hands reached between them and found her breasts, gently squeezing each handful before pinching and rolling her nipples, pleasure and pain, a mixture so sweet that she whimpered in delight. He began pumping his hips, pushing his cock up into her throat, losing his mind as she licked the swollen veins that ran the length of him and then sucked him in again.

Moans and gasps filled the room, growls of hunger echoed, and when he felt her begin to come, that sweet liquid filling his mouth, he buried himself inside her, tongue and cock, and let go. His cum filled her mouth and shot down her throat as his own mouth went wild, frenzied in his need to not let one drop of her sweetness escape his tongue. All he could think was that he wanted more, that he would always want more.

When she raised her head, gasping for air, her next climax ripped through her, and she screamed his name.

Her legs began to tremble and still he continued, coating his thick beard with her honey. When he began to harden again, she begged him to fuck her.

With a final suck and moan of pleasure as he released her clit, and he asked her to beg him again.

"Blaze. Dear God, Blaze, please fuck me. Fuck me hard!"

"You want my cock? You want my cock to fill you? To stretch you? You want my balls slapping against that incredible pussy as I bury myself as hard and deep as I can in you?"

"Yes! Yes!"

They maneuvered their bodies so that he was behind her and when he placed the head of his cock against her, rubbing the tip in her sweetness, coating himself in her arousal, he grabbed a fistful of her hair and yanked her head back making her gasp in anticipation.

"This? You want this cock slammed inside you?"

"Blaze! Yes! Please!"

"Oh, yeah! You better hold on tight, Angel."

With one swift move, he plunged deep, slamming his cock inside her as far as he could, her body swallowing as much of his thick, hard cock as possible. He gasped as the inferno of her pussy set his soul on fire. Buried as deeply as he could go, he pulled out and slammed himself home once more.

When he could take it no longer, he began to move. Hard and fast he fucked her, his body out of control as he set a brutal pace. The harder he went, the faster he went, and the faster he went, the more he tugged on her hair, squeezing and releasing, repeating. When he added in a touch of pain, slapping her ass to spur her on as her body slammed back against his, her guttural cries of "Yes! Fuck, yes, Blaze!" were music to his ears.

Their sweat-slickened bodies worked each other hard as he drove them on a long, hard, punishing ride. Bracing on one arm she reached between her legs to find his sack, and as he pounded her, she fondled it, rolling it across her fingers, squeezing gently, and making him moan in ecstasy. Then she heard it in his breathing, felt it as his balls tightened, as his cock hardened and stilled. And as his body convulsed with his orgasm, he took her with him, both of them groaning in blissful pleasure as they fell once more from the heights of their loving.

"Water...I need water." Lexi lay on the bed gasping for air, Blaze sprawled across her back. Their bodies labored for breath; their hearts raced. Their limbs lay in a tangle and their muscles pulsed in time with their heartbeats.

"I'll get it." He tried to move and found himself too weak. "Just give me a minute to get the feeling back in my legs."

"Stars. I saw the moon and stars. Galaxies. Whole freakin' galaxies. I think my soul left my body. I'm not certain it's back."

"I feel high. Premium weed kind of high. I'm floating." He grunted as he slowly rolled off her body and sat up on the side of the bed. "Want to tell me where all that came from? Not that I'm complaining. Not at all. I just want to make sure that when my feet finally hit the ground that we can reach those galaxies again."

"Ha! I was feeding the chickens..."

"You've fed the chickens before; that's never happened from feeding the chickens before."

She rolled over and poked him in the ribs. "Let me finish. I was feeding the chickens and I got to thinking."

"Not your first time for thinking, either."

She giggled and poked him again, "Stop!"

"I'm done."

"No, you're not, but that's okay."

"So, chickens, food, thinking..."

"As I was thinking I started humming. As I was humming, words started forming. Before I knew it, I was singing. I wrote a song. I wrote my first song since before Jackson died."

He turned to her then, happiness overflowing. "You did? Really? You wrote a song?"

"I did. I wrote a song. I wrote an amazing song. I wrote an amazing song about you. About us. About second chances at life, at love."

"Angel..."

"As soon as I'm sure my legs will hold me, I'm going down to my studio. I need to record it. I need to get it down, to make it real. I mean, it's real, but I need some tangible proof that I did it. That we did it."

Suddenly reenergized, he jumped up, scooped her off the bed, and started out the door and down the stairs.

"What are you doing?" she squealed.

"I'm taking you to your studio." His grin, ear to ear and infectious, had her laughing instantly.

"Blaze! I'm naked!"

"Yes. Yes, you are and so am I."

"Blaze. I can't record while I'm naked."

"Sure, you can."

"Blaze. Stop. Really, I need clothes."

"Not for what I have in mind, you don't"

"What??? But we just... There's no way that you..."

"Angel...I'm going to make sure you are sufficiently inspired." He looked down at her with a wicked gleam in his eyes. "Trust me."

"Oh! Oh, God..."

Chapter Thirteen

Blaze sat on the back deck, beer in hand, and looked across the table at the two men before him as they examined the pile of disabled cameras littering the tabletop, as they discussed and planned. Each man had been with him through some of the hardest times, through some of the most dangerous and intense times he could remember. Military life was never easy and being a part of a small, close-knit unit had brought them together, uniting them in ways that others might never understand.

"I should have known that we were being watched like this. How the hell did I not think of it? How the hell did I miss it? Fuck!"

"Because you've been doing all your thinking with your dick, bro." Blaze flipped off Tank and had the gesture immediately returned.

"We got 'em all. Once we found the first one it was easy to spot the rest. There's been nothing else. Three days and there's been no movement, not even a hint that this person has come back around. We've taken turns on watch, on patrol. We've covered the same ground; we've covered new ground. It's like this guy has just disappeared."

Blaze took a drink as he contemplated. "You guys have mostly been hanging here, but I think we need to spread out. I think we need to split up. I know, somehow, I just know, that it's David. I don't want to leave Lexi, but I have to protect her and as much as I trust you guys, I can't let go of the reins on this one. I have to be the one here with her, or at least until I have no other choice."

"Obviously. Don't worry. We've got you, Blaze. We aren't going to let anything happen to either of you."

"I can't thank you guys enough for your help."

"Brothers forever, man. You're different. You're different with her, and it looks good on you. You've got it bad, my friend."

"She's...everything."

"Understood. So how do you want to make this work?"

"I have some ideas. Lexi isn't going to like any of them, but she isn't going to have much choice. I'm going to fill the Sheriff in, too, because we'll need his help. He isn't going to like it any more than Lexi, but it's what has to be done. It's the only way I can see for us to put all this behind us and get on with our lives."

"We're all ears."

"You guys sure you want in? It might get ugly."

"We're with you all the way."

"Alright. Ok, then. So, here's what I'm thinking…"

Raised voices, angry and hurt, echoed through the house. A door slammed and in the ensuing quiet the unmistakable sound of glass breaking shattered the silence. Moments later Blaze stormed down the stairs and out the front door, duffle bag in hand. Anger and frustration etched the normally smooth lines of his face.

Lexi followed him out the door, hot on his heels. Hurt and disbelief marred her face beneath her own veil of anger.

"How could you do this to me? How could you make me fall for you and then walk away when we hit the first bump in the road? We don't agree on how to handle this situation so you're just going to desert me? What? You can't be in charge so you're going to take your toys and go home? I thought this WAS your home, you bastard!"

"Lexi. Don't. Don't do this. I don't want to leave like this. I don't want to leave you like this. You're making this so much harder than it has to be. If you'd just listen to me, we could put all this in the past; we could move forward in our relationship. But you won't, will you? You've been on your own for so damn long, have become so used to not needing others in your life - have been let down by life for so long, that you can't even fathom depending on anyone.

"You can make that decision and if you do it and can live with it, then so be it. But I have no choice, Lexi. I spent a good part of my life hiding, always looking over my shoulder, always running from one thing to the next. I can't live that way anymore. I want to be with you more than anything I've ever wanted in my life, but I can't go on like this. It's too much. I need some peace. Damn it! I deserve some fucking peace in my life!"

"Well, I guess this is it."

His face, so animated as he'd spoken his needs to the woman he loved, froze then fell, disbelief and rejection hiding the deep hurt beneath. "Yeah. I guess it is."

He turned then and nodded at his friends who'd been waiting by his truck, trying to pretend they weren't witnessing their friend's world fall apart before their eyes. At his nod, they got in the truck and let their own frustrations out in a show of solidarity and support. Blaze winced as one of his friends punched the dashboard and the other hastily ran his hands through his hair as he whispered "fuck" over and over again.

Blaze slammed his truck door as the engine roared to life and without a backward glance, drove down the long driveway for what he feared could be the last time. At the bottom of the drive, he took a left and began working his way down the mountain. He didn't know for certain what was next, but he knew one thing - once again, he was in turmoil.

Tears streaked down Lexi's face as she stood on the front deck watching Blaze disappear down the meandering curves of the drive. When she was certain he was gone, that he wouldn't see her break down, she collapsed, her knees giving out under the weight of her grief. She let it out. The hurt, the anger, the absolute pain she felt at her betrayal, broke the peacefulness of the warm spring day as she screamed in agony.

When at last the screaming stopped and the tears dried up, she sat in silence, her body curled in on itself as she sat with her arms wrapped around her knees. She rocked through the pain and opened herself to the numbness that slowly began to settle in her soul once more.

With an unobstructed view through a high-powered scope, a hard set of eyes watched the scene unfold. Doubt and mistrust had lingered throughout the yelling and screaming of the argument that had unfolded before them right up until the moment they'd seen Lexi crumble in grief and disbelief. And as she'd grieved, they'd watched and waited.

Long after Blaze had disappeared, long after Lexi had gathered herself and returned to the comfort of her home, they'd continued to watch. They'd continued to wait. And as time went on, they began to feel lighter, to feel encouraged. They began to feel hopeful. They began to think that they might, just might, at long last, get exactly what they wanted.

At last, they might finally get what they deserved.

Blaze entered the Sheriff's station by means of the back door, moving quickly at the 'come ahead' motion of the deputy stationed there to await his arrival.

"Blaisure."

"Deputy."

"I sure hope you know what you're doing."

"Me, too."

"We've got ya set up back here. You can see the feed from the cameras. Your guys did a good job angling them just right so that we get good views of the house, the doors. I can only imagine how worried you are, but she should be fine."

"I dropped my guys about a half mile down the mountain. Tank is headed back to Lexi and Viper is making the trek to David's. As soon as I have confirmation that David is out of the house, I'm headed back up." He turned and looked at a map pinned to the office wall. "I'll need you to drop me about here. I'll circle around and head back to Lexi's. Then all I'll be able to do is watch and wait. Kaminski's already on the way up, right?"

"Yeah, he'll be waiting for word on David, too. As soon as he's far enough away the Sheriff's going to try to get David's wife to talk. Then we'll see. We'll just see what's what. For now, how about you fill me in on why you think he'll go to Lexi. What makes you so sure?"

"David has feelings for Lexi; I've seen it in his eyes each and every time I've been around him. He may be married. He may love his wife. But that man wants Lexi, or at the very least, he wants something from Lexi. It's a kind of crazed desperation lurking underneath the normal he projects. I've seen that kind of look before. That kind of crazy? That kind of desperation? It's fucking dangerous. And it's even more dangerous when you have a background like David's.

"So, while my friends and I were planning all of this, we laid a false trail at his feet. When we found the cameras, we also found listening devices. We disabled the cameras to make it appear he'd been found out but left the channels open so he could hear what we were planning. He heard everything we wanted him to hear, and none of it was our true plan.

"The fight Lexi and I had was epic. I swear that woman can do it all. You would have never known she was acting. He'll go to her. Trust me. He'll go. It's just a matter of time."

"Alright. So now we wait. Why don't you go on back to the kitchen? I don't know about you, but I'm a stress eater. I stopped at the diner on my way in and grabbed some comfort food. And there's pie."

"Pie?"

"Yeah, pecan pie."

Blaze chuckled. "Pecan pie. I don't know if that's going to calm me down or hype me up, but I'll never turn down pecan pie."

"Go on then. I'll watch the monitors. Nothing's going to happen to her; we won't let it. I swear we're going to take him down and you two will be able to live in peace. Finally."

When word finally came that David's truck was nowhere in sight of his house, Blaze climbed in the deputy's car and prayed he was doing the right thing, that he hadn't miscalculated, and that this nightmare would be behind them soon.

While they made their way back up the mountain, Lexi, still acting her part for the eyes she knew watched her, poured a glass of wine and curled into the corner of her sofa. She was dazed, red-eyed, and heartbroken. At least the heartbroken part wasn't completely an act, she thought.

She stared down into her glass and thought back over her friendship with David and Melinda. Somehow, even though she knew better, she'd held out hope that Blaze had been wrong. That David wasn't behind all the trouble they'd been having.

But she could see now, it was truly the only thing that made sense. He'd lied to her about his background and knowing that he'd lied about that made her wonder what else he'd lied about. His reactions to Blaze's sudden appearance in her life made it obvious that he wanted something more than friendship from her, but she just didn't know what that "more" was.

Lexi took a sip of her wine as she pondered. Poor Melinda. She couldn't imagine how hurt her friend was going to be when she discovered all that David had done and was doing. Lexi shook her head as she felt sorrow for all that Melinda had already endured.

The poor woman could hardly leave her house without a panic attack. How would she manage once they had David behind bars? Lexi could only imagine just how betrayed Melinda would feel. She just hoped this plan worked and that they'd soon be able to move on with their lives. She despised having this hanging over her and Blaze's relationship.

Lost in thought, she took a drink and almost choked when the knock on her door came. This was it – David had arrived. Her heart hammered in her chest as she tried to catch her breath.

Dear God, she thought, please let this work. With her instincts screaming for her to be cautious, she rose and made her way to the door.

Sheriff Kaminski stood on the front porch of the little house in the clearing trying to catch his breath and doing his best to hold back the tears that had welled in his eyes and threatened to fall because of the scene he'd found waiting for him inside. In all his years on the force he didn't think he'd ever seen anything quite like what he'd just witnessed.

He'd been waiting at a pull-off for his opportunity, and when he'd received word that David's truck wasn't on the property, he'd driven the last mile of the climb up to the house and parked his car. He'd waited for a moment after pulling into the drive, hoping that Melinda Osborne would get curious and come out to speak with him.

When she didn't, he made his way to the door and knocked. There had been no answer, so he'd knocked again, calling out to her that he'd come to check on her, to talk with her. And again, there was no answer. The base of his neck had begun to tingle at that moment, a sign that something was seriously wrong with the situation.

He'd come prepared, warrant in hand, and under the authority of the State of West Virginia, he'd broken down the door and began his search. The living room and kitchen had shown no signs of Melinda and he'd begun to search the rest of the house.

What he'd found had left him sick to his stomach. Though he knew at that moment that Blaze had been correct, that something definitely had been off about David, about the Osbornes, he couldn't help but feel some amount of sympathy for them and what they'd endured.

He'd found nothing unusual in the house other than an organization that left no doubt that someone was OCD about the placement of their belongings. Room after room he'd looked in had been spotless with very few personal items lying around. Everything had been placed precisely, lined up perfectly, and there'd been no "homey" touches that he associated with a house being more than a structure for shelter. No throw pillows, no knick-knacks, no dust collectors like what his wife had decorated their own home with.

The final room he'd checked had been the room that was to have been the baby's nursery. This was the only room that had any frills, any extras, and seeing the differences between the baby's room and the rest of the house, gave him chills.

He'd walked in the doorway of the room and stopped, quickly glancing around. He'd started to walk back out, but something had told him that he needed to investigate further, and trusting his gut, he decided to check it out.

He'd wandered fully into the room and begun circling the perimeter, not finding what was making him wary. It wasn't until he stepped up to the baby's crib and looked inside that his heart had simply sunk in his chest.

What would have been an adorable little room painted a soft blue and holding all the needs of a newborn baby, was instead a macabre tomb for the tiny skeleton wrapped in a blue blanket and placed lovingly in the baby's crib.

Knowing he'd been on the verge of losing it, he'd quickly gone to the front porch to gulp down as much fresh air as his burning lungs would hold. And as he'd waited for his backup to arrive, he'd grieved for the parents who'd never been given a chance to see their child grow and become. He felt sympathy for them and sadness for the child who'd never been given a chance at life, who hadn't been allowed to rest in peace.

In all his years as a cop, as a detective, he didn't think he'd ever seen something quite as heartbreaking as what he'd just witnessed.

As he stood on the porch and looked out over the Osborne's yard, his senses were tuned in tightly to his surroundings. And when he heard the shuffle and click of a shotgun being cocked, he knew he was in trouble.

"Sheriff. I'm going to ask you to get in your car and drive away. There's nothing here that concerns you." The deep voice surprised him, and his mind began to race as he quickly figured out that it hadn't been David that had left their property."

"David. If you'd put that gun down, I'd like to talk with you." He knew he had to get him talking, had to try to get through to him. The Osbornes needed help and he wanted to get that for them. But if he refused, if he fought him, David would be the one to pay the ultimate price.

"That's not going to happen, Sheriff."

"David, you need help. I want to get you the help you need. If we can just talk for a bit, I'll see what I can do."

"Again, that's not going to happen, Sheriff. You keep sticking your nose in where it doesn't belong. I thought for sure you'd have taken the hint when Melinda blew out that tire and sent you rolling down the mountain, but you just don't seem to give up.

"You're as bad as Blaze. We'd thought he was gone when he left in the winter, but he just had to come back. I thought that when I'd shot him, he'd get the hint, but not even taking a bullet would make him leave Lexi. Now, Sheriff, I really don't want to hurt you, but if you don't start minding your own business and get in that car and drive off my property real quick like, I'm going to have to shoot you, too."

"I'm not going anywhere, David. I want to help."

"Well, then have it your way." He sensed the shifting of the gun as David aimed it a little higher and he closed his eyes as he waited for the inevitable. When the gunshot pierced the stillness surrounding the house, his heart leaped and he dropped to the porch floor, seeking cover as quickly as he could. He heard the quiet gasp, the clatter of the gun as it fell, and he looked back in time to see David's body as it fell in a heap onto the hard wooden floor of the porch.

The Sheriff scurried over to where he lay to begin chest compressions, but he knew by the blank look in his open eyes that there was no hope.

A moment later his deputy, accompanied by Blaze's friend, Viper, walked up on the porch. Incredulity with an undercurrent of sadness surrounded them as they began going through the details of what happened and the gruesome scene in the nursery.

An ambulance was called. An alert was sent out to everyone. And they waited.

Lexi opened the door and was shocked and confused to see Melinda standing there. She tried her best to greet her as if nothing was wrong, but with Melinda's appearance, she knew things weren't going as Blaze had hoped and planned.

"Melinda? What...what are you doing here?" Lexi wasn't sure what to think or how to handle things as Melinda pushed her way into the house, past Lexi, and into the living room where she immediately made herself comfortable on the sofa.

Trying once again to act normal as her mind started screaming at her about the danger she was facing, Lexi anxiously scanned the front yard as she closed the door. And as she turned around and saw the crazed look on her friend's face, she knew that she'd been lied to repeatedly.

Melinda, it seemed, wasn't actually suffering from agoraphobia. No, the wildness, the insanity in her eyes told Lexi all she needed to know.

"Well, I'm feeling so much better, and I hadn't seen you in so long that I thought I'd stop by." She grinned, "And, David has been telling me about this new man in your life. I'd love to meet him! Where exactly is he? I didn't see any extra cars when I pulled up."

"Oh, well, he's gone to town to pick up a few things."

"Really?"

"Yeah. He'll probably be back any minute."

"Are you alright? You seem a little off... Why, Lexi! Have you been crying?" The sweetness in Melinda's mountain twang made Lexi cringe.

"I'm fine. Just fine."

"Are you sure? You know, it's been a long time since you've been down to the house to sit for a spell. Why don't I take you down there and I'll throw some brownies in the oven? We can have us a glass of wine and something sweet while we catch up!"

"Oh, I would love to do that, but I just don't feel like going anywhere right now. Maybe another time?"

"Come on. It'll be fun!" The pleasing tone of her voice slowly crept toward demanding, and Lexi began to realize just how seriously wrong this whole crazy plan could go if she made one bad move.

And with that realization flashing like a neon sign in front of her, she began to lie, telling Melinda anything she could think of to stall and give Blaze a little more time to arrive and help her handle the madness she now faced.

When the call came from the Sheriff updating him on what had happened at the Osborne house, the unease that Blaze had been feeling about the whole situation, increased. He hadn't really counted on Melinda being involved – not if she truly suffered from agoraphobia. But now he knew that she did actually suffer from mental illness – it just wasn't as they'd been led to believe.

By the time he'd reached the house, David's truck had already been in the drive. Blaze had been watching, carefully hidden while he'd awaited word from the Sheriff. When he'd gotten the call, he'd begun to pray that all his years of training had prepared him for whatever awaited him inside Lexi's home. Insanity came in all forms, he thought.

With thoughts of getting to Lexi and making sure she was safe first and foremost in his mind, he sprang into action.

As he approached the house, he saw no movement and heard no noise. A quick glance across the driveway told him Tank was taking care of his part of the plan. David's truck sat in the drive with four flat tires and Blaze's friend was in the process of letting the air out of Lexi's tires as an extra bit of insurance. Even if things went horribly wrong, Melinda would not slip out of their grasp easily.

Quickly and quietly, he snuck onto the porch and eased his way over to the door, his Glock drawn, finger on the trigger, and ready for whatever he might encounter. He peeked in the decorative window and when he did, his blood ran cold. He froze in his tracks as he watched a new nightmare unfold before him.

Melinda, her insanity clear and evident on her face, stalked Lexi as she backed her way out of the living room and into the kitchen. Blaze turned his head quickly, and catching Tank's eye, motioned him toward the back of the house. His friend began to stealthily make his way to the back deck and Blaze prepared to make a move.

The trap was set now and there was no way that he was going to let this opportunity slip through his fingers. One way or another he was determined to get to Lexi and keep her from harm.

"Melinda, I really think you should go now."

"Why? What's wrong?"

"It's just that I...I'm not feeling the best right now."

"Oh, now Lexi. Don't lie to me."

"I'm not! And, Blaze, well, he'll be back soon and...

"Stop. I know he's gone. He's gone and he's not coming back. I saw that fight you two had, and I heard every word. But you don't have to worry. David and I are going to take real good care of you. We're going to be one big happy family. Come with me, Lexi. Come on home with me so you can see how good it's going to be. We've got everything all set up and ready for you. You'll see."

"Melinda, I don't know what you're talking about. You and David are good friends, but I don't understand what you mean about being family."

"Well, see, since we lost the baby, I, well...I can't have any more children. We want kids. You can help us, Lexi. You can help us have children."

Lexi's mouth fell open in shock as the horror at what Melinda was suggesting crossed her face. It was worse, so much worse than what they'd anticipated. "Oh, Melinda. I'm sorry. I'm sorry that the two of you can't have children, but I can't do what you want me to do. I can't help you have children. I won't."

Rage at Lexi's defiance poured from her body, and she made a lunge at Lexi to try to capture her. Lexi side-stepped and Melinda, not anticipating her quick move, stumbled into the kitchen, catching herself on the counter before she could fall. "Now, Lexi. You don't know what you're saying. We'd be a perfect family. You can give us the children we want. We'll take real good care of you, I promise. We have everything all set up!

"David said he'd make sure that I got a baby – as many babies as I want! He said that you're perfect for carrying our children. So young and healthy!

"Now, don't make me mad, Lexi. You've never seen me mad, and you probably wouldn't like it. I don't want to upset you. It isn't good for the baby."

"There is no baby, Melinda! And I'm not going to have David's baby!"

Melinda shook her head as if she were trying to clear her thoughts. "It will be OUR baby, Lexi. We'll have us a boy and a girl, and we might have another just for the hell of it. We'll be the perfect family." Melinda lunged for her again and this time Lexi wasn't quick enough. She screamed as she was grabbed, kicking and fighting against her captor as hard as she could until she managed to slip out of her grasp.

At that moment, Blaze burst through the front door, gun drawn. Melinda turned toward the door at the intrusion, taking her attention away from Lexi. When she saw Blaze, she lost it and with a growl of impatience and a curse for her foiled plans, she turned and began to run toward the back door.

Lexi, witnessing all of this in what felt like slow motion, took matters into her own hands. Heart racing, she looked around quickly for some kind of weapon and seeing her possible salvation, reached for the cast iron skillet sitting on the stovetop. She yelled Melinda's name to get her attention, stopping her in her tracks.

It felt as if time stood still and when it did, she took her chance. With a swing worthy of the big leagues, she brought the skillet up, hitting Melinda squarely on the side of her head.

Stunned, Melinda's body stumbled and then collapsed onto the kitchen floor. In shock, Lexi dropped the skillet and covered her face with her hands, horrified at what she'd had to do to someone she'd once considered a friend.

Blaze ran to her and gathered her close, burying her face against his hard chest to comfort her, to ease his mind, and to protect her from the view of Melinda as she lay sprawled across the kitchen floor. He looked over the top of her head at his friend as he walked through the back door and nodded for him to go check on the lifeless form of Lexi's intruder.

"She's still breathing, Blaze. Just knocked the fuck out."

"Tie her up, Tank. The Sheriff will be here soon."

"Don't worry. I've got it covered."

"Lexi? Angel? Look at me." But she kept her face buried against his chest. "Come on, Angel. Look up here." Slowly she raised her head and searched his face, looked into the eyes of the man she loved. "You're okay. You're okay, Angel. And Melinda's just knocked out. Alright? You knocked her out, but other than a possible concussion, she'll be fine."

At that moment her body began to shake uncontrollably. "Oh, God. Okay, Lexi. C'mon." Blaze scooped her up and carried her to the living room. Sitting down with her on the sofa, he held on tightly, comforting them both, waiting for her body and mind to catch up to the reality that the worst of the whole situation was behind them.

"It's all over, Angel. The Sheriff will be here in a couple of minutes, and he's going to take her away." He tilted her head up then and looked deeply into her eyes. "You, my love, were fabulous."

"Is it really over?"

"Yes. She is going to be locked away for a very, very long time. You're never going to have to see either of them again."

"Blaze?"

"Yeah?"

"I need a drink."

He laughed, and feeling relief that she was coming back to herself, crushed his lips against hers.

Epilogue

"I'm having such a hard time believing that she was that insane, that they were both that crazy."

A couple of hours had passed, and the crime scene unit had finished at both locations. Several bombs had been found and diffused at the Osborne's home. Traps that had been set up around the property with the intent to seriously harm and possibly even kill an intruder, had been found and disabled. David Osborne's lifeless body had been removed from the property and the remains of their still-born baby had been taken by the local coroner at the same time.

Melinda had been taken in handcuffs to the hospital for an exam and then to the psychiatric ward for evaluation. Ballistics would soon match the spent bullets, from the shooting in town, as well as the one dislodged from the tire after the Sheriff's accident, with those located in the Osbourne house. Melinda would soon be locked behind bars, and it wouldn't be long until she was convicted and never allowed to see the light of day again.

A celebratory shot of whiskey had been shared with Blaze's friends before they'd gone their separate ways, and Blaze and Lexi now sat in her living room discussing the case with the Sheriff, trying to take in all that had happened.

"When I searched the property, I found their whole plan laid out in their shed outback. The surveillance system was in there, and we'll be able to match all that up with the cameras you and your guys found, Blaze. The shooting in town? They were trying to scare you off and in case that didn't work, they had a plan to take you out. That was well documented, too.

"They had planned to use you, Lexi. They wanted you to carry a baby for them because Melinda couldn't any longer. They had planned to kidnap you, rape you, impregnate you, and keep you captive until the baby arrived.

"We found a small cabin tucked way back on the edge of their property line. They had a room all set up for you. Damn it, there were even shackles on the wall and a hospital bed. There were surgical tools and drugs

– everything they would need should worse come to worse, or should you need any persuading.

"Forensics is still going over the cabin, but I don't think you were their first, Lexi. I think they've abducted other women at some point. We'll be calling in cadaver dogs to search the property. I hope I'm not right, but I have this nagging suspicion that we've just scratched the surface of what we're going to find.

"Your instincts were pretty much on target, Blaze, and thank God for that. I suppose that when the baby died, something just snapped in both of them. The parent in me almost wants to feel sorry for them. Almost.

"I kind of feel that if their baby hadn't died that none of this would have happened. But at the same time, I feel like if it hadn't been the baby, something else would have happened, would have pushed them. It was only a matter of time. You know, sometimes, those who act the sanest are the ones you really have to watch out for."

"I don't suppose I'd ever really thought about it, but that makes a weird kind of sense." Lexi laughed and looked over at Blaze with a mischievous grin. "Does that mean we're actually sane?"

"You're a funny woman."

"I try."

"The two of you remind me of me and my wife twenty years ago. Oh, to be that young and carefree again. Don't take a moment of your time together for granted, you two. And speaking of my wife, I'd probably better be heading home. It's been one long-ass day."

"Thanks for all you did, Sheriff."

"Oh, I think maybe you better be thanking Blaze and his friends. Brilliant, cunning, and devious minds, all of you. We probably wouldn't have figured this out so quickly and couldn't have covered as much ground as we did if it hadn't been for the three of you."

Blaze grinned at the backhanded compliment. "We're just glad that it's over so that we can move on."

"Speaking of moving on, I do have one thing I'd like you to think about."

"What's that?" Blaze asked.

"Well, I don't know what your plans are, but I assume you're going to be staying in the area. With your military background and that brilliant mind, you'd be an excellent addition to the Sheriff's office."

"Oh, huh. Well, I..."

"Just think about it, son. You're young and you've got plenty of time to make a decision." He looked over at Lexi and smiled from ear to ear, "But let me tell you, there are some decisions I wouldn't wait too long on if you get my drift. There are some of those decisions you need to make and jump on as soon as you can. Time moves too swiftly to let some opportunities pass you by, to waste precious moments while you're waiting for the perfect one." With that, he stood to leave. "I'll see myself out," and with a wink, he was gone.

"Well, huh. I don't know that I ever would have thought about joining the police force. I'll have to think about it."

"I'm going to tell you what a very wise person once told me. I want you to do and be whatever makes you comfortable, whatever gives you the most pleasure, whatever makes you the happiest. It's your decision and I will support you either way."

"A very wise person?"

"Wise, handsome, sexy, mouth-watering, brilliant. Sexy. Did I say sexy?"

"Come here." He pulled her into his lap and pressed his lips to hers. "Lexi. You know those decisions that the Sheriff was talking about?"

"Yeah."

"I need to ask you something and I need you to make a decision. And I want you to remember what I told you not that long ago about the question."

She smiled up at him as her heart leaped. "Go ahead, I'm ready. Ask. Ask me because you need to. Ask me because you need to say the words, want to say the words. But I'm going to go ahead and tell you my answer now."

"Oh really? And just what is your answer, Angel?"

"Yes. Without a doubt, my answer is yes."

To be continued...

More by Dawn Love

Meet the Cassidy Brothers! These sexy, single brothers may not be looking for their happily ever after, but fate has other ideas. Join Cade, Cameron, Colton, Calvin, and Colby as their destinies are revealed!

Across the Hall

Across the Road

Across the Lane

Across the Field

Across the Miles

Acknowledgments

This book may have been my most difficult to write, to date. There's so much of myself buried in these words that I still find parts of it very difficult to read. And while my story is far different than Lexi's, I can honestly say that fate has a way of stepping in and redirecting our lives when we least expect it.

Without a doubt, the first person I have to thank is Matthew Hosea. Yes, fate stepped in the day I found you on Instagram, and I'm so very thankful. You have helped to open doors for me that I'm not certain I would have ever attempted to open on my own. Sharing your knowledge of the book world, and introducing me to some amazing photographers and cover models has been such a blessing. Thank you for making me laugh, for sharing parts of yourself with me that others may only catch a brief glimpse of, and for being such an amazing person to work with. I know you will see bits of yourself in this book and I hope I gave justice to your personality and character. I promise you that if I get the chance, I will bake you a pecan pie one day.

To the Goldens – Czermak and Angel: Thank you both for sharing your expertise and experience. Contracts, trademarks, copyrights, marketing, publishing – I could go on and on. I've learned, and continue to learn so much from both of you.

Thank you to my Beta and ARC readers: Thank you for your feedback and your reviews. You are an invaluable part of this process and I appreciate you more than you will ever know.

Many thanks to my friends and family for your constant support and understanding, especially when I lose my mind (however temporary) over my writing. I could not do this without you.

About the Author

Dawn Love was born in Mayfield, Kentucky, and spent the first twenty-six years of her life there. Always a creative person and an avid reader, she began writing stories for her own entertainment as a teen, and her love of writing continued to grow into adulthood. Meeting the love of her life brought many changes, including moving 900 miles away from home and settling on the Delmarva Peninsula where she resides on her 50-acre farm. Now the mother of two teenagers, she spends her free time creating the characters and stories of her fantasies. She also writes an internationally read Blog where she gives her readers a glimpse into the craziness of her day-to-day life, her mind, and all that the world throws her way.

Made in the USA
Middletown, DE
04 December 2022